Jules Arentz is a native Californian. She comes from a large family with a love for wayward animals. She and her beloved husband of twenty years chose not to have children because they share the joy of being Aunt and Uncle to over thirty children. Jules lives a quiet life with her husband and enjoys visiting family, traveling and reading. *The Turning Page* is her first book.

The Turning Page

Jules Arentz

The Turning Page

Vanguard Press

VANGUARD PAPERBACK

© Copyright 2024
Jules Arentz

The right of Jules Arentz to be identified as author of
this work has been asserted by them in accordance with the
Copyright, Designs and Patents Act 1988.

All Rights Reserved

No reproduction, copy or transmission of this publication
may be made without written permission.
No paragraph of this publication may be reproduced,
copied or transmitted save with the written permission of the
publisher, or in accordance with the provisions
of the Copyright Act 1956 (as amended).

Any person who commits any unauthorised act in relation to
this publication may be liable to criminal
prosecution and civil claims for damages.

A CIP catalogue record for this title is
available from the British Library.

ISBN 978 1 83794 112 4

This is a work of fiction. Names, characters, businesses, places, events and incidents are either the product of the author's imagination or used in a fictitious manner. Any resemblance to actual persons, living or dead, or actual events is purely coincidental.

Vanguard Press is an imprint of
Pegasus Elliot Mackenzie Publishers Ltd.
www.pegasuspublishers.com

First Published in 2024

Vanguard Press
Sheraton House Castle Park
Cambridge England

Printed & Bound in Great Britain

For my husband, who gently pushed me to keep going and follow this dream.

1

"Ma'am, you will need to remove your jacket before you go through." *What? Oh.*

"Um, Sure." There I was, lost in thought again. I looked apologetically at the airport security guard pointing at my tray of items and quickly moved to the side. I folded my jacket over the tray and placed it on the belt for screening, then I stepped into the next line. *I can't believe I am doing this!* This is the last thing anyone would expect from me, including me.

I took a deep breath after I made it through security at LAX. Following the crowd, I found my gate. Then I grabbed a cup of tea and a new book from the newsstand. Scanning the waiting area, I spotted an empty seat between a tall man on his phone and a mom with an infant sleeping in a car seat in front of her. They both offered a smile and a nod when I pointed to the seat, so I settled in.

One overnight flight to Dublin, just under eleven hours to overthink all the things that could go wrong. My teeth worried my lip. Who would have thought? Me, dependable, stable, make no waves, plain Jayne Sinclair would be going on an adventure. Even my name is plain.

Mom and Dad couldn't agree on a name, so they didn't even try for a middle name when they had me. I would imagine wonderful middle names for myself growing up that I could go by instead of Jayne, but Mom would hear none of it. At least they threw in a Y so it wasn't so boring. They figured it out for my little sister, Samantha Rose, five years later, but I remained as boring as could be. Perhaps the name fits.

One night a few months back, on a whim and probably one too many glasses of wine, I sent in an application to an ad I saw on social media: "Six months in Ireland, helping to run a bookstore, room and board." Okay, so the bookworm in me probably had more to do with it than the wine. I could live in a bookstore and now I get to live above one for six months.

They accepted my application long after I had completely forgotten about it. After I got over the shock, it was just a matter of applying for a Working Holiday Authorization to stay for more than ninety days and asking for a six-month leave of absence from the job I've had for nine years. I can't even believe my boss said yes. I packed my bags before I thought about it too much and changed my mind. Now here I am, in all the hustle and bustle of LAX. Every penny I have accounted for and accessible if I need it for the next six months in a country I visited once, for two weeks right out of high school.

I tell myself it's an adventure of a lifetime. One I can tell my kids; I was once wild and crazy enough to travel halfway around the world, leave it all behind and just see where it takes me. Or I could tell them the truth; that it was an opportunity of a lifetime, but that my job was waiting for me when I returned, and my sister was renting my apartment for me while I was gone. I suppose it will depend on what kind of kids I have. Best not to think about that though, I'm twenty-eight-years-old, single, and have no prospects… kids are not really in my future at this point. Once, I had a pregnancy scare from my one and only one-night-stand. Thinking back, I'm so glad it was a false positive. Never again would I be that foolish.

Announcements to board the plane brought me out of my thoughts. I scanned my ticket and shuffled slowly down the narrow aisle of the plane. I looked around and couldn't believe my luck. The flight attendant announced that the flight wasn't completely full, and after a bit of shuffling from the person sitting next to me, I found I had my own little two-seat section in economy all to myself. The flight attendants did their thing while I settled in for the flight. E-reader, new book, music, snacks, and hopefully, one small nap and I would be there. Maybe a glass or two of wine when the flight attendants came by? No turning back now. One more deep breath. Here goes nothing!

***

A fairly uneventful, albeit cramped, night with my books, snacks, and my wine. Even with my two seats, it was a long flight in a tiny space. The mom and car seat baby were my neighbors across the aisle. The baby had done well and only got fussy a few times throughout the night. Not bad for a first flight and being so little, but mom looked frazzled.

Morning came and I moved around and stretched as passengers jockeyed for position to use the tiny restrooms on the plane. I grabbed my chance, and with a toothbrush and small toiletry bag in hand, I prepared to make myself look somewhat presentable. I quickly ran a brush through my long, straight, brown hair and popped it into a travel braid. I've had long hair my whole life, thanks to my mom not letting me cut it until I was eighteen. After that, I was too afraid to cut it too short. My biggest hair change-up after I turned eighteen was to cut bangs. They were a disaster. I got an 'I told you so' from my mom and never did anything like that again. I tried to smooth out the flyaways to no avail then ran my toothbrush around my mouth. Then I pinched my cheeks and swiped on a bit of mascara. It was good enough. At least I looked alive again.

We landed safely and there was a buzz of excitement from the passengers as they gathered their items. I still couldn't believe I'd done this all on my own. On my walk to baggage claim, feeling a little like cattle, I logged into the airport Wi-Fi and made the obligatory phone calls to my mom, my dad, and my sister, letting them know I landed safely. I re-explained to my mother that I would be fine, and as soon as I was settled, I would call her and give her the book shop phone number, address, and even my GPS tracking if it would make her feel better so she could get a hold of me.

Mom worried out loud, "What are we going to do without you for six months?" I'm the one she depends on to keep her sane. I again told her we would get through it and then rushed to get off the phone, so I could snag my bag from baggage claim and get on the first of a couple of buses for the long ride to Cong. My first bus ride took about an hour. It was from Dublin Airport to the main train station. I watched the grey city of Dublin pass by the windows of the bus. I waited for my stop, the last stop for the bus, Heuston Station. I gathered my things in a rush and exited the bus, trying to stay out of other people's way. Still organizing myself, almost dropping my phone, I hurried into the train station. I got swept up in the crowd but managed to find my train and fight through the throngs of people to get to it. Settling in and getting comfortable on the train to Galway, I cursed myself for not flying into Shannon Airport but it was cheaper, and I did just sort of quit my job.

The train was surprisingly nice and I had more room than I did on the plane. Once out of the city, I watched this new, very green world fly by. I relaxed into my seat and watched the train chase the sun. The sky was a vibrant blue, peeking out through the clouds one minute and dark and stormy the next. It slowly switched back and forth a few times during the two-and-a-half-hour ride. The green was almost unexplainable, especially since I had spent all of my life in Southern California. Everything at home was mostly brown... even in the springtime, with only a few green trees here and there. Even the buildings and houses seem to be a shade of brown or gray, but here, it's a patchwork quilt of greens. There must be every shade of green you can think of, all spotted with little white sheep with black faces and feet everywhere. It was absolutely breathtaking. The houses here only added more color to the landscape as they popped up here and there along the way.

    I arrived at Galway Station. It was significantly calmer than the airport. I found the Left Luggage Office and paid two pounds fifty to have them hold my big bag while I spent my three-hour layover wandering the streets of Galway before my last bus would take me to Cong. It started sprinkling again so I made sure I had my Boston Scally cap (a souvenir from my longest trip away from home since my trip to Ireland ten years ago) and my raincoat before I left. I double-checked my backpack for my umbrella too. I walked out of the train station just as the sun peeked out from under a cloud and headed towards Eyre Square. It was a green space in the middle of the city center with tall flag poles that ran down one side of it. There was a full arch rainbow in the sky over the green space. The sprinkles stopped just as quickly as they had started and the rainbow faded as I made another left and turned to go down Williams Street, which turned into High Street then Quay Street. It's about half a mile stretch of stores and restaurants that went all the way to the river. My legs woke up and tingled, letting me know I had sat too long. I lengthened my stride, working out the kinks as I passed pubs, shops, and restaurants. After I had made my way down to the River Corrib, I noticed a tea place. Just as I stepped towards the door, I could feel the raindrops hit my face. I figured it was a good time for me to stop and get a bite before I headed back to the station.

The front window had little teacups hanging from strings. There were baskets hanging on either side, and a window box full of greenery, spotted with flowers. The sign outside assured me that I would be stepping into The Original Irish Tea Shop and that I did. The smell of freshly-baked everything was heavy in the air as I stepped inside. The cinnamon and nutmeg reminded me of my grandma's house when I was little. The tantalizing smell of tea brought a smile to my face.

The small, round woman behind the counter greeted me and told me her name was Joanne. She assured me the weather would change again before I knew it and offered me a pot of tea. I gladly accepted and asked for a spiced scone with cream and jam to go with it. She pointed me to a small, empty table while she busied herself behind the counter. I sat down with all my things and made myself comfortable. The room was small with mismatched chairs and tables all covered in pretty linens.

There were a few customers at other tables and a little girl running around with her doll in a matching dress. I caught her eye and smiled. She and her doll waved at me before she ran back to her table. Joanne sat everything down in front of me on mismatched floral China. She showed me the triple sand timers and told me not to touch my tea until the green sand ran out. Joanne offered that their soup of the day was cream of vegetable and convinced me it was the best in town. So, as she went to get me a cup of soup with some brown bread and butter, I started on my scone. The whole room was covered in floral everything, from tablecloths to curtains, and nothing was the same pattern. It was eclectic and exactly how I imagined a tea shop should look. Everything was delicious! The scone was soft and still warm from the oven, the tea was strong and flavorful, and it was the best soup I had ever had in this town, so I couldn't argue with her.

    I paid my bill and thanked Joanne for everything. Waving goodbye to the little girl and her doll, I ducked out into the mist and made my way back to the train station. I passed by all the shops again, lingering at the windows. I hoped that, at some point, I would be able to come back while I was here to look through every last one of them.

    I collected my bag from the station and pulled my ticket out of my wallet. I watched as my next and last bus pulled in and a few passengers got on. By then, it was early evening and I had about an hour bus ride into Cong. I settled in with a full stomach and my e-reader, getting lost in the latest Nora Roberts while the countryside passed me by when I glanced up from time to time. I checked for my paperwork and directions on how to get to the bookstore once I got off the bus as we got close.

Cong is a tiny little tourist town. It's only a couple of streets long by a few streets wide. I'm not sure you could get lost there if you tried. Unless you went into the forest, which I did plan to do, with my books, on my first day off. Cong's claim to fame was that it was the filming location for *The Quiet Man*, a movie with John Wayne and Maureen O'Hara. As the bus pulled through the town and around to the bus stop, we passed a statue of John holding Maureen in the famous pose from the movie. That movie was a favorite of mine growing up, so I looked forward to exploring the little town.

The bus finally got through the narrow cobblestone streets and stopped. All the passengers made their way off. There weren't very many of us when you compared it to the buses at home, but everyone seemed friendly. It was still early spring so the tourist rush would be coming in a couple of weeks. I got my bag and backpack and made my way up the street to the bookshop, The Turning Page, Home of Rare and Recent Books.

2

The streets were lined with what looked like one solid building and each section was painted a different color for the different shops and homes as you went. Each window and door was adorned with window boxes and hanging flower pots. The colors were almost overwhelming. *How can there be so much color here?* Then, as if the sky was answering my unspoken question, it started to drizzle. I quickly stepped into The Turning Page. I looked around, breathing in the smell. It felt like home. I've always loved bookstores and libraries. I could spend days in them, or in this case, six months.

The bells on the door signaled to the man behind the counter that I had arrived. He greeted me kindly and told me his name was Thomas O'Bryan. He was tall and thin with red hair that had silver peppered through it. His face was round with a red beard and his blue eyes sparkled with mischief. He asked me to call him Tom after I introduced myself. Tom then introduced me to his wife, Maeve. We had spoken on the phone before when they accepted my application. They explained that they owned the shop and would be very glad of the help when the tourist season started. Maeve was much shorter and a little stouter with wild auburn hair that had flashes of silver throughout. The unruly curls looked hard to tame in this weather. She had soft hazel eyes and freckles on her nose and cheeks that made her look younger than she was. Tom and Maeve were around the age of my parents, and I warmed to them immediately. Maeve fussed about and told Tom to carry my bag to my room while she closed the store. I tried to carry it myself, but Tom would hear none of it.

"You wouldn't be trying to get me in trouble with the missus now, would you?" he asked not yielding the bag. I released my bag to his capable hands and followed him toward the spiral staircase in the back of the shop. He removed the chain that hung across the opening, and we climbed our way up two floors. Tom explained as we made it to the second level, that he and Maeve had a bedroom on the first floor along with the kitchen and dining room, so if I need anything, I would know where to find them. Apparently, they number the floors differently in Ireland than they do in California. Our first floor is their ground floor and our second floor is their first. That would take some getting used to.

We arrived at the top of the staircase. I told myself the stairs would be good for me, but I was so glad Tom had my suitcase. The top floor was where my room would be with a bathroom to myself. There was also a small sitting room and closet for my things. Tom explained that the room used to be his son's room, but he had moved out some time ago and worked at the castle. Ashford Castle was not far from the town and Sean would come to visit when he had the time. Sean worked with the falcons at the castle. I could tell Tom was very proud of him.

The room we entered had an almost young boy's room feel to it. The walls were light blue with a full-size walnut-colored wood bed and dresser. There was a small lamp and a soft white comforter with blue pillows. The wool, Aran knit sweater style throw on the bottom corner of the bed made me smile. I brought one of those back when I visited this country for the first time, and I loved it. Tom pointed at the throw,

"The wood stove takes some time to get running in the morning and the heat takes a bit longer to make its way up here, so the throw is just in case you catch a chill."

The room had a small window that looked out over the front entrance of the bookshop. I could see the shops on the other side of the street through the shop windows and a sliver of the river that ran behind the little town. Everything else was green trees and gray skies. I loved all of it!

Tom left me to get settled and told me Maeve pushed supper back a bit in case I was hungry when I arrived. He said it would be ready at eight p.m. and asked if I would like to join them. I nodded and smiled. As he headed down to help Maeve close up, I looked around the room and started unpacking. There were a few shelves on the walls and a couple of pictures. One was of Tom and Maeve when they were younger and a small, red-headed little boy with a giant smile. *That must be Sean.* There were some children's books on the shelves and a small soccer trophy from ages ago, First Place Team, The Rovers, Sean O'Bryan. I wondered if Maeve would come in and reminisce when they didn't have anyone staying.

There was a small book on the dresser with the Wi-Fi code on the front. I opened the book and found little journal entries of the past employees they've had here. I had set it aside to read later tonight and made a mental note to make sure I add a couple of my own entries. I entered the Wi-Fi password into my phone and sent my mom and sister a text with a picture of my new bed. I finished getting myself unpacked and went to take a shower before dinner. Once I was dressed and presentable, I walked down the spiral staircase, and since I had some time, I went all the way down to the ground floor to wander the store and better acquaint myself with it.

The store was packed with books and trinkets for book lovers. I immediately wanted one of everything. I hoped the little bit of spending money they give me for working would pay for all the things I already wanted to buy. I wandered around a bit, taking everything in. I picked up cherished books I've read and found new books to add to my ever-growing "to be read" list.

Maeve called out that supper was ready. I headed back upstairs to the second, er… first floor. The smell of Guinness stew made my mouth water. Maeve gave me a quick tour of the little kitchen.

"Everything is available to you if you wish it, and if there is something that you would like, you need only ask."

I smiled my thanks and we sat at a tiny round table with an Irish linen tablecloth that had shamrock accents on it. Tom served up the stew and Maeve handed me a piece of warm bread. They held hands and invited me to say Grace with them. I was raised Catholic, but I've been out of practice for a while. I placed my hands in theirs and bowed my head. It was short and sweet without being understated. They jumped right into conversation and the meal, asking me about my life back home and about my job as we ate. There wasn't much to tell, really.

"I am the oldest daughter of divorced parents and have a younger sister who is twenty-three. My job is as a secretary and assistant for the owner of a company that sells stationary. I don't even have a dog. It's just me and my books in my apartment which my sister, Samantha, and her boyfriend, Jake, are renting as a test run for when she decides to move out of mom's house and live with him. My mom is busy at home as a seamstress. She works with a couple of the local dry cleaners in the area to do the tailoring when they have a need. The house is small but currently has more animals than humans have ever lived there. Mom and Sam, we only call her Samantha when she is in trouble, love animals and they take in all the strays they can find. Dogs, cats, rabbits, tortoises, fish, ducks, geese, you name it, they probably have it or want it. It's probably why I never got around to getting a pet when I moved out. No real need because I can just go visit when I want."

Tom and Maeve took turns telling stories of the town and themselves. Maeve would bat at Tom with the dish towel when he got his details mixed up or told stories she said, "just weren't true". He would just smile and wink at me. Tom and Maeve met in high school in Galway. They married a few years after graduation and bought The Turning Page from a little old couple, the Kellys, when they retired. They had Sean a year later and he grew up in Cong. The castle at Ashford was well known for its horseback riding and its birds of prey. They offered outings with the falcons and you could watch them fly through the forest and then land on your glove. Sean was one of the handlers for the birds and he helped with the horses too.

Maeve and Tom like to get away in the spring and again in the mid-summer so, after Sean moved out and had his own job to do, they needed someone to come and learn the shop and keep it open while they took holidays. I was to learn for about a month and then they would be off to Naples for a couple of weeks. After that, they had time set aside for the Faroe Islands in late summer. They loved living in the small town but they liked to see other places, and now that they were older and Sean could take care of himself, they could take holidays and go see places. Tom said each time he comes back liking his little town even more. Maeve is the traveler; Tom seemed to be along for the ride.

We finished dinner, followed it up with a glass or two of Jameson whiskey, and then I offered to do the dishes which made Tom smile, but Maeve wouldn't allow it. She shuffled me off to bed, saying I must be tired from my trip, which I was. As I walked slowly to the staircase, I saw that Tom was starting the dishes. *No wonder he smiled*. Maeve said that tomorrow was a day for me to wander, get acclimated with the time change and see the town. She said I could start at the shop first thing the following day. I got to my room, sent a goodnight text to my mom and Sam, and was asleep before my head hit the pillow.

3

The next morning, I woke up at three a.m. Wide awake thanks to jet lag. I wandered around my room quietly and decided to read through some of the journal entries. It looked like the O'Bryan's have had spring and summer help for about eight or nine years. Most of the entries are just thanking them for the great time the helper had, but a few tell of places they explored and the locations they ate. It was helpful for planning my day later. I picked up my phone and googled Ashford Castle. I checked out a map of the grounds and the surrounding areas trying to orient myself. Ashford Castle was large but the grounds were even more expansive. Lots of land and forests surround it and there's a paved one-way road that leads to Cong.

There were a lot of locations in Cong that reflected the town's claim to fame, *The Quiet Man*. There was a museum, a hotel, the old abbey that I remembered from the movie and the pub, Pat Cohan's, which if the movie is to be believed, it's pronounced Co-Han. I couldn't wait to visit them all. I decided to bide my time and wait for sunrise reading my book. I don't remember how far I got so I will have to re-read all of it but I fell asleep at some point and didn't wake up until nine a.m.

The Turning Page was open by the time I got dressed but there weren't any customers. I could hear Tom whistling down in the shop and Maeve was in the kitchen. They had been up for a while and had already eaten breakfast. She looked at me knowingly and pointed to some scones and a teapot. I smiled and made my way to the table. Bless her, the tea was strong and the scones were still warm. I nursed my jet lag and enjoyed every warm sip of tea with milk and sugar. It was so soothing. Maeve finished cleaning up and placed a small brown bag in front of me.

"Snacks for the day and dinner will be around seven tonight if you'll be wanting to join us again," she said as she headed downstairs to the shop. I savored my last bite of scone and downed the rest of my tea. I washed my dishes and then went up to grab my backpack. After a quick peek in the brown bag, I placed my snacks in my backpack next to my e-reader. It was cheese, fruit, and bread. I filled up my travel water bottle and headed downstairs, excited to start my day.

I found Tom wandering the Irish history section, dusting the books and shelves. "You'll have an umbrella and a raincoat with you?" he questioned. I nodded and smiled at his very dad-like question. I turned and thanked Maeve for the snacks and stepped out onto the street. Kegs lined the street in front of the pub and all the shops were open. The sky promised a sunny day but I knew that wouldn't hold all day. Maeve came out the front door with a small box in her hand,

"Och, Jayne!" she said, "You've had a package arrive just yesterday and I forgot it entirely." I walked back inside, knowing what it was. I opened the box and pulled out my rented hotspot. I put all the packaging in the trash and attached the hotspot to my travel charging block. I quickly connected my phone to the hotspot and I was off with a wave.

I walked up and down all the streets just taking everything in. Making sure I knew where the restaurant, the pub, and the convenience store at the petrol station all were. The rest of the shops were filled with Irish knick-knacks, Aran sweaters, and souvenirs. The owners and shop staff were friendly. Most asked if I was here to help at The Turning Page. Apparently, nothing goes unnoticed in a small town. It didn't take long to see the whole little town so I walked toward the old abbey.

The abbey was made of grey stone and the ruins were mostly intact. There were several pointed archways that could have been windows or doorways. There was a small cemetery with elaborate headstones and a larger one on the side of the abbey, near the street. I spent some time reading the headstones that hadn't faded with time, finding the dates surreal and fascinating. Some recently interred residents had more contemporary-looking headstones that both fit and were out of place in the cemetery. I followed a long corridor out to a beautifully manicured, green lawn and the town disappeared. Before me was a forest full of every shade of green I could ever imagine. Even the bark on the trees was covered in green moss. I followed a path out toward the river. There was an old stone bridge with an open gate on either end. I made my way past a small building with no roof on the edge of the river before I crossed the bridge. According to the sign, it was an old fishing house for the monks at the abbey when it was in use. The sound of the river and the breeze traveling through the trees made the area feel so peaceful. I wondered if it would be this peaceful when the tourists started to arrive.

I decided to keep following the trail that led into the forest. As I wandered into the trees, I didn't have to go far before I found another building. This one was unique. It was square with a flat clear glass roof. The walls were grey stone pillars with turquoise glass chunks scattered throughout. The pillars had clear glass panes between them and there were low stone benches inside. There weren't any signs around it but it was so beautiful. It almost looked like a place of prayer. I made a mental note to come back and read there. The location was perfect and I could stay out of the rain when it came. I wandered around in the woods and watched the light dance through the trees when the leaves quivered with excitement as the breeze blew through them. I stepped carefully around roots and fallen trees, occasionally catching a drip from early morning rain that made its way through the canopy. Small paths led off the main trail, deeper into the forest. The main trail was well-worn with some soggy areas where the trees thinned, and every now and then, it would become grass patches where the sunlight could peek through.

After wandering the forest for an hour or two, I headed back, across the river to the abbey and turned right. I followed the trail that led to the castle. The trail was a one-way road. It was wide and paved but flanked on both sides by forest and the river. It was a fairly easy walk and the trees were old and beautiful. I could hear the birds singing happy songs as I traveled down the road. I passed by an older couple holding hands and smiled at them. The woman smiled back and the man tipped his hat and said hello.

As I made my way to the castle, I walked past an old church, St. Mary's, with a very tall steeple, a small guard booth, and tons of trees and green grass patches. A light drizzle started just as I rounded the bend and Ashford Castle came into view. I pulled out my umbrella and walked over a large stone bridge. The water was flowing quickly and the sound the river made was soothing. I stopped in the middle of the bridge and hopped once, jumping the imaginary line from County Mayo to County Galway, laughing to myself. Once through the archway, Ashford Castle stood before me in all her glory. It was a beautifully large castle, made of grey stones complete with crenellations and turrets. It was magnificent.

I decided that I would go inside the castle at a later date. The drizzle wasn't so bad and the sound of the river and the fresh air called to me. I stopped under another stone archway long enough to pull out my snacks that

Maeve had given me and continued to walk the path around the castle. The grounds were extensive and well-groomed. I passed several people out for walks including a woman pushing a stroller and a little boy on a bike with one training wheel. The woman would call for him to turn around when he got too far ahead. He seemed to be practicing with only one training wheel so right turns were easy but left turns were a bit tricky. He fell just in front of me but wasn't hurt. I dusted him off and helped him back on his bike. He rode straight for her arms. I waved as I walked by and the woman smiled back and thanked me for helping him back on his bike.

 I munched on my pear and then moved on to the cheese and bread. It was a great snack to get me through the rest of my walk. A short time later, I came to a clearing with a sign for the equestrian center. There was a large, fenced area with horse jumps and I could see archery targets in the distance. I could hear the horses in the stables. Growing up, my uncle had a farm so I loved horses. They both fascinated and scared me. I walked around the building and peeked inside. The smells reminded me of the farm. It was so busy inside. There were stable hands moving from stall to stall, some mucking out the stalls and others grooming the horses. I decided to come back later when it wasn't so busy so I turned around to go back the way I came and ran right into a person. As I stumbled back, they reached out and caught my arm. We righted ourselves before we could hit the ground apologizing to each other. I looked up, blushing with embarrassment and stopped mid-apology.

Sean O'Bryan stood right in front of me. He was the spitting image of the little boy in the picture, just older with a red beard trimmed close to his face. His smile was exactly the same. He was dressed in a long sleeve green button down, a pair of jeans and work boots. The green in his shirt made his eyes look green, though I assume they changed color based on what he was wearing, like my sister, Sam. I blurted out his name and he was caught off-guard. He removed his cap and asked if we'd met before. Rambling more than I had hoped to, I explained that I was working for his parents for the spring and summer and I recognized him from his pictures. I told him my name and he said he remembered his mom telling him about me. He smiled and asked if I would like a tour. Not wanting to be a bother, I tried coming up with an excuse, but he ushered me into the stables and started his tour with the first horse. She was a beautiful little grey horse with darker grey freckles all over. Her name was Millie. She was very sweet and liked that I still had pear juice on my hands.

Just as we started to move to the next horse, a woman at the end of the stables stepped out of a doorway and yelled down to Sean,

"George is waiting for you at the falconry." Sean apologized for having to cut the tour short and then asked if I had been to see the falconry yet. When I shook my head, he offered to take me there. We hopped on a large golf cart and headed out. Sean spoke of his job and the birds he worked with. He was a perfect tour guide pointing things out along the way. We passed The Old School and turned left then we followed a tree-lined path and turned left again onto a dirt path that brought us to a door with a sign for the falconry. I was going to need a map to get back to Cong.

He hopped out of the cart and gestured for me to follow. We walked through the door then turned and went into a small lobby area. Behind the counter was a white-haired older man wearing coveralls and mud boots. They shook hands and Sean introduced me to George. He asked if I had Sinclair relatives in Northern Ireland. I told him I wasn't aware of any and that my family is in California but the Irish in me comes from my mother's side. Her maiden name was Kendrick. George started to tell a tale of someone he knew long ago with that surname, but Sean gently interrupted him as he winked at me. Sean reminded George that he called him back to the falconry for something. George hopped up out of his seat and he spoke so fast I didn't quite catch everything as he sped away and Sean and I followed. Something about a fern and hatchlings.

We came to a stop in front of a metal enclosure. Inside was a brown hawk with her feathers all fluffed up, sitting on a nest. Apparently, George had heard one of her eggs had hatched and they were waiting to see if her second egg had hatched as well. Sean looked at me and explained that the hawk's name was Fern and that she was a new mom, then told me I was lucky to be here for this. It was fascinating to watch him work with her. He put a gloved hand inside the enclosure and offered some bits of chicken meat. As she grabbed for them, she moved just enough for us to see the first hatchling, all fuzz and wrinkly skin. Sean said Fern was doing very well and that they would keep an eye on her and the new babies. He said all they could do was wait and see. I was amazed. He just had his hand right next to a new nesting mother. He told me she was a sweetheart of a bird and she was going to make a great new mum.

George went back to the lobby and Sean showed me around the falconry as methodically and practiced as any tour guide. He pointed to each cage and told me little stories about each bird. There were all different kinds. They even had a couple of owls. I was beyond impressed with his job. He offered to take me on a hawk walk during my stay with his parents. I smiled but didn't really answer. Horses scared me a bit because of their size, but birds of prey are a whole new kind of uneasiness.

I looked at my watch and couldn't believe the time. We went back to the lobby but I had to start heading back if I didn't want to walk through the woods alone, in the dark. I said my thank yous, my goodbyes, and a promise or two about coming back. After a very long set of directions from George on how to get to the front of the castle, I walked out of the falconry. Waiting until I was out of view from the windows, I pulled out my phone and plugged in my destination. Glad my portable Wi-Fi was working well, I headed to the castle. I hadn't gotten very far when I heard a golf cart coming up behind me. Sean pulled up next to me and said it wouldn't be very hospitable of him to make me walk all the way back. He offered to drive me to Cong if I went with him to put away the cart and get his lorry. He said he called his mom and told her he would bring me home and stay for dinner. Maeve was thrilled.

We drove back the way we had come and dropped the cart off at a shed near the equestrian center. Then we walked a little further into the tree line where there was a small staff parking lot. Sean had a little blue pickup truck that he called a lorry. Once I was inside his truck, I could smell his cologne combined with the smell of the farm. Sean said his house was just outside of town and asked if it was all right if we went by so he could run in and get a clean shirt and a bottle of wine to take for dinner. I wasn't going to argue so we drove out Ashford Castle Drive. We passed a golf course and drove through the front gate. A few minutes down the road, Sean turned left and drove down a small lane. We pulled into his driveway, and so it didn't get awkward, I offered to stay in the truck while he ran inside. He smiled, said he would return in just a bit, and walked quickly to the house. It was a cute little house, not terribly small. The house was whitewashed with dark blue shutters and front door. The house had trees around it and a small front yard with a garden peeking out from the side of the house. It looked like it had just been planted or was waiting for seeds. The rock wall surrounding it was covered in hedgerows of berry bushes.

Sean came out of the house in a crisp blue button-down dress shirt, clean jeans, boots, and a new, nicer cap. His eyes were gray now just like Sam's would be. He had a bottle of wine in each hand. He opened the door and asked if I minded while handing me the bottles. I took them both and set them in my lap saying, "Not at all." One was white and the other was a red blend. I hadn't heard of either winery.

We weren't very far from Cong so our conversation on the drive was short. He asked what I did back in California and what had made me send in my application. I pointed to the bottles of wine on my lap and said,

"Their California friends might have had something to do with it." He laughed and said,

"Well, now, I suppose we have something to toast to tonight."

We arrived a bit early. The shop was still open but Maeve and Tom were getting ready to close. Maeve had started the roasted potatoes and the pork loin in the kitchen. You could smell them cooking down in the shop. There were a couple of customers left, both were locals. When Sean walked in, he was greeted with handshakes and hugs. Maeve introduced me to the customers, Katherine and Donnie Armstrong. Maeve said they were regulars and always looking for something new. Katherine and Donnie were husband and wife, married for forty-five years. Katherine was tall and slender with curly, shoulder-length, salt and paprika-colored hair. She wore an embroidered sweater, cream with navy flowers, and navy trousers with matching shoes and purse. Donnie was taller than her by a couple of inches. His hair was grey under his cap. He wore jeans and a pullover, dark grey sweater. Donnie had their rain jackets over his arm. He wore small, square glasses on the end of his nose, and I caught him smiling at Katherine when she wasn't looking. They enjoyed reading but had different tastes when it came to it. Donnie loved war books and liked non-fiction. Katherine was interested in romance novels and said, with a smile, that it was because Donnie was never romantic. I stifled a laugh. They made their purchases and said their goodbyes. Donnie helped Katherine into her jacket and held the door for her, they left holding hands as they walked down the street. I smiled to myself.

  Maeve shooed Sean and me upstairs to the kitchen so she and Tom could finish closing up. Sean pulled out four wine glasses and opened the bottles. I opted for the white to start. He handed me a glass, we toasted to the bottle of wine that got me here, and I sat at the table. Maeve came up and Sean handed her a glass of white as well. She checked the oven and then came to sit by me at the table. I asked if there was anything I could help with and she batted at me, saying Sean and Tom could handle the setting of the table and that I would have plenty of time to help while I was here. Tom came up and Sean set two more glasses of white wine on the table. Then told his dad with a pat on his shoulder,

  "We've dinner service to do when the timer goes off so don't get too comfortable." Tom took a sip of wine and then gathered plates and napkins. He and Sean set the table as the timer went off. Sean pulled dinner out of the oven and let the pork rest while he put everything else on the table. Tom sliced the pork loin after the rest of the table was set and then brought it over to the table. We served ourselves, passing the dishes and talked about our day.

Maeve was a wonderful cook and she had an icebox cake in the freezer for dessert. We all had a glass of red after dinner and then Tom brought out a little port wine to go with dessert. Sean stretched and leaned back in his chair. Maeve yelled at him for putting the chair on two legs. Sean smiled, lowering the chair back on all fours. A little while later, he said he needed to get home. Maeve mentioned quietly that it was because he didn't want to do the dishes. I smiled, said goodnight, and thanked him for the tour and for the wine. He offered that, anytime they gave me a day off, I was welcome at the castle. He gave me a wink which combined with the wine had me blushing. Sean smiled at his mom and she gave him a great big hug. He shook his father's hand and that turned into a hug too. Tom walked him down and I helped Maeve with the dishes. With a tear in her eye, Maeve said,

"I miss him but I get to see him more than my friends see their children so I can't really complain." She asked how my mom handled the news of my trip, it being for so long and all. I smiled gently and said,

"About as well as you would handle it if Sean were to take a trip for six months." She smiled to herself and said,

"It's a mother's job to worry about her children." I agreed, mentally telling myself to figure out the time difference and make sure I call.

Tom returned, conveniently, just as we finished the last dish. We talked for a few minutes about my schedule and the schedule of the shop. In the winter, it was open when they wanted it open, as many of the shops and restaurants in small towns will do, but while I was there, they would keep a regular schedule, especially when the tourists start to arrive. They were open every day but would usually open late when they went to church and they would post a sign when they weren't there. For my schedule, they want the store to be open by nine a.m. and close at six p.m. I could take my lunch when it was convenient while they were here and when they were gone, I would keep my lunch in the small fridge behind the counter, closing when I needed to use the restroom if there were no customers. Tomorrow I would start with Maeve and she would show me how to use the register. Tom would show me how to place special orders and what methods they used to keep the shop clean and tidy after. Then they would show me where they keep their stock and the books and items they have on hold. It would be very exciting to see how the whole operation worked.

I couldn't believe what a great first day I had. I said my good nights and went upstairs to the sitting room. I cleaned out my backpack, put everything away, and took a shower. The time difference was eight hours so at ten p.m. it was only two p.m. at home. I sent my sister a text to see if she had a minute to video chat. Not a minute later she was calling me. I pressed the button and she squealed. She wanted all the details of my first day at the shop but didn't let me speak. She went right into telling me she was enjoying her time at my apartment, but they missed the animals. I told her my apartment doesn't allow animals and that I better not get a call from the owner because she tried to sneak one or more in. She promised she would try not to. I laughed and told her she could always hang out at home and then go to the apartment later in the evenings. She agreed.

I started to tell her about my day, she interrupted me to tell me I would never find a guy if I spent all day with my nose in a book. I continued as if she hadn't interrupted, and she practically came through the phone when I described Sean. I had to turn down the speaker on my phone so Maeve and Tom couldn't hear her. I told her he was very handsome but I wouldn't see him much for the rest of the week so I would have to see what vibe I got the next time I ran into him. My sister was always so quick to fall in love. Probably why she picked up every stray animal she could find. I loved it about her but it could be overwhelming when she imagined me getting married to every guy I talked about. I told her it was late here, and I wanted to get a quick chat in with Mom before I headed to bed. She was heading into work so she had to go too. I didn't bother to text my mom. I just video-called her. She answered on the fourth ring. I imagined her rummaging for her phone in her purse and her fumbling to get to the button before I hung up. You could hear the relief in her voice when she said my name. She asked how I was and how my time had been so far. She said I'd been gone too long already and asked when I was coming home. She was half serious. I smiled and asked how the animals were. She said Sam had plans to come by in the mornings and in the evening to help her get everyone fed. They are all doing well except Sam's cat, Lucy. She missed Sam at night so Lucy and Mom's dog, Lady, had to figure out how they were planning to share the end of Mom's bed. Lady was Mom's dog; a stray poodle mix she found one night in a rainstorm. I told her that they would work it out. She asked me what time it was in Cong and I told her it was about ten-thirty p.m. She told me to get to bed. I laughed and thought of saying something about being twenty-eight and going to bed when I decided, but I was tired so I told her I would head to bed. I told her I loved her and wished her goodnight. Then I set my alarm, crawled into bed and turned off the light. That night I dreamt of horses, a falcon, and a red-headed man named Sean. *Thanks so much, little sis!*

4

I woke up the next morning around five a.m., shook my head, told my bladder *no* and went back to sleep. The next time I woke up was to my alarm, feeling rested. I gathered my things and took a quick, wake-me-up shower. I finished getting ready and met Maeve and Tom in the kitchen. It looked like it was going to be a slow start to the morning. Tom was reading the papers and Maeve was checking emails. There was a pot of oatmeal and toast and jam on the sideboard. Maeve said good morning and pointed to the pot. I smiled and said good morning, grabbing a bowl and a cup for tea. Tom poured my cup of tea and topped off their cups. We sat in blissful silence, enjoying the quiet morning. I was reading my emails on my phone when Maeve looked at her watch.

She said, "It's about time to clean up and head down." Tom folded his newspaper back up and started to collect the dishes. As I moved to help, Maeve caught my attention and gestured for me to follow, leaving Tom to clean up. We went downstairs and opened the front door to a drizzly morning but you could tell the sun was trying to shine. There was a small rainbow in the distance. She walked behind the counter and said, "It's good for Tom to do the clean-up now and again." Even though he had done it quite often since I arrived. It seemed he might be showing off a bit and Maeve was taking full advantage.

Maeve showed me the Point-of-Sale system that they used. It was really easy. Scan barcodes, if they wouldn't scan then type them in, if they came up wrong or not at all just enter the info and use the miscellaneous button but add a note with the title and author or what the item was. She said when they got any customers I could try it out. She showed me where they keep the extra change for the register and where the deposit goes at night after closing. She said she would show me the closing procedure this evening.

Tom came down the spiral staircase whistling. He wandered over and kissed Maeve on the cheek and thanked her for breakfast. She blushed slightly and shooed the two of us off to the computer down on the other end of the counter. Tom showed me the websites and the companies they use for special orders. I took notes on a small pad and left them in the drawer below the keyboard. It seemed pretty straight forward. Tom said before Sean left to work outside the bookstore, he had made sure they knew how to place the orders and wanted it to be as uncomplicated as possible. He said sometimes they get people that want to sell their books to the store. They keep a small book with rare requests, and only if the person is selling one of the requested books, would they buy it, but in the book was the highest price the customer was willing to pay for it, so that was all they could offer for the book. If a book came in, we would call the customer to verify they still wanted it and the price they were willing to pay before they bought any used books. If the customer was selling books that they didn't need, there were a few locations in the larger cities that bought books. There was also a list of local churches that would take donated books.

We moved on to the backstock and hold items. There was a small room in the back of the store near the staircase. The room was mostly shelves. Tom explained they don't keep a lot of backstock and that the room was mostly for holds but there were a few items that tourists love that they kept on hand so they didn't sell out. The hold section had baskets on the shelves. They were arranged in alphabetical order by the last name of the customer with bright yellow sticky notes. I noticed the Armstrongs had their own basket and the sticky note was taped to it, making it almost permanent. It made me smile. I imagined they weren't exaggerating when they said they were always in the shop and wondered what their house looked like.

I heard the bell indicating that someone had opened the door and Tom and I went back towards the front of the shop. Maeve was welcoming the two ladies. They said they had just come in to look around and wander the shop. Maeve told them to just ask if they needed anything, gesturing to Tom and me. The ladies smiled and started to browse. Maeve pulled out dusters, spray bottles, and small cloths, handing them to the two of us. She was wiping down the counter and Tom and I moved methodically around the shop and through the aisles, dusting books and wiping shelves and tables.

 For lunch, Maeve sent me up to the kitchen; she had set out a charcuterie-type lunch for us to share. She joined me a few minutes later and we ate first while Tom covered the store. Then it was Tom's turn to eat. Customers came and went; I used the register without issue. We cleaned and straightened, restocking what was available. I helped an older woman named Phyllis and her nephew, Arthur, look for a new book for her. She was delighted with my suggestion and said she would see me next week. Arthur wheeled Phyllis's wheelchair down the road and back to her home. Maeve worked on an order for Phyllis, tracking down the other two books in the series and showed me how while she explained that Phyllis was a regular customer. She and her husband, Harold, used to come in all the time for new books. Harold passed away about five years ago. They were married for sixty-six years. Phyllis now had nurse caretakers at home, but once a week, her nephew came and brought her to the bookshop and to the store at the petrol station to get sweets without the nurses finding out. Maeve explained that Phyllis liked murder mysteries and that she was always looking for new ones. The nurses read to her so she got through about one book a week which worked out perfectly for her nephew's visits. I made a note on my phone to look up other murder mysteries for her so that when she finished the series I started her on, I would have new suggestions.

It was a busy and productive day. The sun was setting and it filled the shop window with an orange glow. The rain had let up earlier in the afternoon and the evening was clear and calm. Maeve showed me how to close out the register but she hadn't had a chance to start dinner, so we closed up the shop and walked down a few businesses to have dinner at Pat Cohan's Pub.

According to Tom, a few of the locals were in for the night along with some new faces. The inside of the pub looked just like the movie. They even had the old taps at the bar. Jerry was the bartender and server. He said hello to Maeve and Tom, smiled at me and pointed to an empty table. He called from behind the bar and asked what we were drinking. I opted for Guinness and Maeve and Tom agreed so, a few minutes later, three Guinnesses showed up at the table with the menus. The chalkboard sign on the wall said the soup of the day was cream of vegetable. Sold! Tom got the pot roast and Maeve ordered the fish. Dinner was delicious, my soup came with warm brown bread and butter. We ordered the cheese board for dessert. It came out just as a couple of customers pulled out some instruments. A fiddle and a tin whistle. The music started, more rounds of beer were ordered and the crowd started singing. Hands clapping and foot stomping joined the music. It was quite a scene. I tapped out after my third pint of beer, fearing a hangover in the morning. Switching to water, I watched the evening unfold. A few of the customers started to dance. Maeve pointed at a couple and said their names were Grant and Molly Campbell. They were regular customers. Molly had just announced her pregnancy a week or so ago and you could see that she was just starting to show. The couple noticed the O'Bryans and motioned for Maeve and Tom to join them, so they stood and took a turn around the room. They sat down after the song ended with smiles and a light flush. They finished off their beers and said they were going to call it a night. Maeve handed me a key to the bookstore. She said it was mine to keep until I had to go home and said to enjoy the rest of the night.

They left the bar after paying the tab and headed home. I waited a few minutes but didn't want to get swept away in the music and agree to dance with someone, so I made my way out into the evening air. I could hear the river a couple of streets away. I walked out to the water and found a small bridge with a sign that had a line down the middle. One side said County Mayo and the other said County Galway. I wandered to the middle of the bridge and put one foot on each side. Laughing to myself for being in two places at once.

The moon was full so its reflection sparkled on the water. It was so peaceful. The wind blew softly, and I could hear the music from the pub slightly. I took a deep breath. *I only have six months here. It's been two days and I never want to leave.* I walked the streets of Cong for a little bit but it started to rain and I didn't bring my rain jacket. I walked quickly to The Turning Page; I was pretty wet by the time I made it through the door. I took off my sweatshirt and dried off what I could before I got too close to any books. I tried to be as quiet as possible heading upstairs. I stopped on the second floor. I could hear Tom snoring. I was so glad I couldn't hear him upstairs and wondered how Maeve got any sleep. I went upstairs and hung my wet clothes in the bathroom, making a mental note to ask Maeve where I can do my laundry in the morning. I threw on my pajamas and crawled into bed. I sent my mom a quick text and quickly fell asleep.

5

The next few weeks went by slowly and steadily, though St. Patrick's Day was quite lively even for this sleepy little town and the stories about the parades and the four-day festival in Dublin sounded amazing. It was definitely a great time to visit Ireland. Sean came by a couple of times to visit and took everyone out to dinner one evening. I was getting really good at using the register and Tom had me doing all the special orders. They left me to run the store a few times while they ran errands and they actually took a day off to go into Galway for an overnight date. I got a day off here and there and spent it in the woods with my book, picnic-style. I made it over to the glass-roofed structure in the forest twice and did some reading. I loved that place. It was so peaceful.

Tomorrow was my next day off and I decided to go back to Ashford Castle. I packed a few snacks in my backpack, including an apple I cut up for Millie and any of the other horses I might meet on my visit. Looking at the map on my phone, I found an old tower on the grounds called Guinness Tower. That was one of my destinations for the day. Maeve gave me Sean's phone number and let him know I was planning on visiting the castle. He said if he didn't have a busy schedule tomorrow that he would look out for me.

I set out my clothes so I could get an early start and made sure I had layers for when the weather changed. I threw my Scally Cap on the pile for good measure and texted my sister to see how my apartment was doing as I climbed into bed. She video-called me and we talked about our week. She told me that the apartment was great but that the neighbor below had a flooded bathroom when a pipe broke. Thank goodness my apartment was on the second floor. The owners were going to have all the pipes checked so they may be without water for a couple of days, but only during the day while she was at work. I reminded her that there shouldn't be any pets in my apartment and she promised me that she hadn't brought any to stay the night. She said she might have brought Lucy over on her day off but took her back home before the evening. I rolled my eyes and changed the subject. I told her my plans for tomorrow and she got very excited. She asked if Sean was going to be there and I told her that he does work there and he doesn't have the day off, so it is probable that I would see him. She asked if we were dating yet. I rolled my eyes at her again. I asked her how Jake was. She told me he was fine and they were doing well living together. They may start looking for apartments so I could have mine back when I got home. I was excited for her. I told her she had to plan a trip out to Ireland. It's magical here. She laughed and said she might if she ever got better about saving money. I told her I had to go and get some sleep. She giggled and told me to dream of tall, red heads. I rolled my eyes yet again, said I loved her and hung up. I turned off my light and stared up into the darkness. I couldn't wait for tomorrow.

6

Morning came and I got up with the first bits of light. I dressed quickly and braided my hair. I had put on a little makeup and a few quick swipes of mascara. I grabbed my backpack, and as quietly as I could, made my way down the staircase. *Have you ever noticed when you are trying to be quiet, you are actually louder than you would have been if you had just been quick?* Maeve had the kitchen tidy so I tried not to make a mess. I put the kettle on and noticed some pastries from yesterday in the glass bell cloche dish on the table. I snagged two, one for now and one with my tea. I poured the hot water into my travel mug and grabbed an extra napkin. I wrote a small note on the pad of paper next to the fridge and gathered my things. I headed to the door and put the pastry in my mouth so I could unlock and lock the door. Then I was off toward Ashford.

It was a quiet walk through the forest on the road. The birds were chirping and I could hear the little creatures scurrying in the underbrush. The river flowed with a tinkling sound as I wound my way along it towards the castle. The canopy changed from high to low and back again. I heard the wind whip through the trees and then calm again, almost as if the forest was taking deep breaths. I saw someone ahead of me and recognized George from behind. I caught up quickly and tried not to scare him. He turned with a smile and asked why I was heading to the castle so early. His shift didn't even start for an hour but it took time for him to walk there. I explained that I planned on exploring the forest and was going to look for Guinness Tower before it got busy with the tourists that had arrived over the last week. He smiled at me and asked how my stay had been and if they had kept me all these weeks without a day off to come to visit. I smiled and told him I had a few days off but I used them to explore the rest of the area before I came back to the castle.

We chatted away on the walk to the castle and I offered him the pastry I had brought with me. He split it in half and shared it back with me. I smiled. He told me of the hawks and what had happened since I was last there. Fern and her two babies were doing great. They should start learning to fly in about a month. There was a foal born just last week. They named her Colleen. He said she was chestnut brown with a reddish-brown mane. He invited me to the stables and introduced me when we got to their stall. She was in with her mother, Cara. Cara was a beautiful rich chocolate brown, very tall, and almost regal. Baby Colleen was spindly and adorable. I pulled out a piece of cut apple for Cara and Colleen licked my fingers after her mother delicately took the apple from my hand. It was quiet in the stables. No one had really shown up yet. I stopped by Millie's stall and gave her a few pieces of apple. She munched away at them and made noises of satisfaction.

George laughed and said, "You know the way to that one's heart!" He asked if I would like a ride to the trail for Guinness Tower since I brought him breakfast. I agreed and we walked to get the golf cart from the shed. He drove slowly to keep the both of us from catching a chill in the dewy morning air. We chatted about the bookstore some more and about the hawks.

We pulled up to a crossroads and George pointed the way, giving more description than actual directions. I thanked him for the ride and he thanked me for the morning company. I had set off along the trail and I followed George's "directions". I saw the landmarks he spoke of, a metal gazebo, a handwritten wood sign, a tree laying down that was bigger around than I could hug, and a stone sign that said, "Built by Guinness 1864". The tower was massive, at least to me. It was no Ashford but a single square tower that stood five stories high, wrapped in tendrils of ivy. I grabbed my flashlight and my phone out of my pack and snapped a few pictures before I went in. I made sure I was in a few for my mom who swore that if there was no one in the picture then it was just a postcard.

The tower had one stone spiral staircase on the inside, with nine window cut-ins on the way up. There was one small room at the top as well as roof access. I, of course, headed for the roof first, passing each window quickly on the way up. The windows were like arrow slits. Just small rectangles of light, each facing a different direction. I realized all the windows and door openings had a pointed arch and weren't really rectangles, making them a bit unique. I got to the top of the tower, passing the one room. There was no door to it or to the roof. It was just open. I walked out onto the roof and there was a short wall all the way around the square roof. I took a deep breath and walked to the edge. I looked out and was almost even with the treetops. I looked down and couldn't believe how high up I was. There was thin metal fencing to keep people from falling, that ran the full length of the roof. I'm not afraid of heights but it made me feel a little better that it was there. The birds in the area were singing their good morning songs and the sky was now light enough to read. I dropped my bag and pulled out a yoga mat I had cut in half and a small blanket. I picked a corner and set up my things. Sitting picnic-style on the yoga mat with my back against the wall, with the blanket on my lap, I opened my book. Enjoying the quiet and the small sounds of nature, I dove into my book. Looking up occasionally as a bird flew by or landed on the roof. It was so peaceful.

7

About an hour later, the sky was lighter but the sun was behind the clouds. Now wrapped up in the blanket to ward off the chill from the stone, I felt the first drops of the next storm land on my cheek. I unwrapped myself and went down one floor to the room. It was lighter now and I could see relatively well without the flashlight. I laid the yoga mat on the windowsill and wrapped the blanket over my shoulders. I put my bag on the floor and sat in the window looking out at the green. I watched the rain fall and it got heavy enough that the water was dripping down the staircase. It started dripping through the cracks in the stone above me so I moved slightly to avoid getting wet. I decided to wait out the rain then I could head to the falconry and see the birds before I explored the inside of Ashford.

Another hour or so went by but the rain hadn't gotten any lighter and I wondered how long it would take. Just as I finished my chapter and resigned myself to the fact that I was just going to have to walk in the rain with my umbrella, I heard a golf cart pulling up. I looked out the window and realized I was facing the wrong side of the building, so I hopped down and headed to the other side of the room. The golf cart was there just outside the arched doorway but it was empty. I heard a man's voice call my name. It was Sean. I called down the staircase as I gathered my things. He came up to meet me halfway.

"What are you doing here?" I asked.

"Looking for you," he said with a smile. The staircase was very small. I stood on the step above him, almost at eye level with him. He said George mentioned our morning and that he had dropped me at the trailhead for Guinness Tower. When the rain hadn't let up, he figured he would see if I was okay. I told him I had just finished reading and taking photos and was about to head back. He grinned, tipping his hat and offered me a chivalrous ride to the falconry. He put his hand out and I placed my hand in his.

He chuckled, "I was asking for your pack so I could carry it down the stairs for you, but if you want to hold my hand too that would be grand."

Blushing with embarrassment, I stepped back forgetting I was on the stairs and fell right on my butt. He laughed and so did I. *What else could I do?* He offered to carry me down if I needed him to. I thanked him sarcastically and he reached out to help me up. *Why was I always so clumsy around him?* He took my bag and held my hand as we made our way down to the front door. We both stared at the sky like we could time our run between the drops to the cart. Then he asked if I was ready. I nodded once and he took off pulling me behind him. We loaded ourselves into the cart and he helped me zip down one of the plastic sides that were on it. He reached again for my hand as he started the cart, grinning and saying he wouldn't want me to fall out. I didn't know whether to be mad, happy or nervous. I was all of those and embarrassed. I scowled at him and then smiled because his grin never wavered.

We drove to the falconry, both quite pleased with the silence and our hands touching. Just as we pulled up, he asked what my plans were for the rest of the day. I told him I was hoping to see the birds again and then I planned on making my way to the castle to see the inside. He said he would be glad to show me the birds again as his morning appointments had been cancelled because of the rain. I agreed. We walked past all the cages. He reminded me of the names, and apart from Fern, I confessed I had forgotten most of them.

We stopped in front of Fern's enclosure and she was looking uncomfortable. She reminded me of a very patient mother waiting for her children to take a nap. I smiled and she seemed to sigh and fluffed up her wings. She got up out of the nest and there were two fluff balls with a couple of real feathers moving around and very alert. They bent and stretched their little wings, moving about the nest. Sean said their names were Fiona and Fergus and that you could tell them apart by the shape of their face. I couldn't tell the difference, but I let that pass unsaid.

Sean asked if I was ready to hold a bird. I pointed at the babies and said Fern would probably not be very happy with me. He laughed and said he wasn't talking about the babies. He pointed the way and told me about Archimedes, a short-eared owl they picked up as a rescue from Northern Ireland. His previous owner found him as an owlet and hand-raised him. When the owner had to move, he couldn't take him so they called and asked if the falconry would take and care for him. Sean said he was very sweet and affectionate and perfect for first-timers, as Archimedes liked to be petted and most first-timers couldn't help but want to touch the birds.

8

We got to a large enclosure that had large beams along the ceiling. Sean unlocked the door and stepped inside. I swallowed hard, took a deep breath, and followed him inside. Sean reached for my hand and pulled me close. He slid a thick leather glove on my hand and turned me around. He stood behind me holding my arm up and bent. He whistled lightly and I heard the flapping of wings. I froze and Sean squeezed my shoulders with encouragement. Out of the corner of the enclosure came this large brown and white owl. He landed right on my very shaky arm and Sean brought my arm down to a more comfortable position. He introduced us and stroked Archimedes' chest with the back of his bare finger. Archimedes made almost a cooing sound and leaned into Sean's touch. He was beautiful. He had a heart-shaped face with dark inset feathers at the edges of his large golden eyes. He had a cute wide-eyed expression that looked almost like he was waiting for more affection. I reached a very shaky hand up slowly and brought my hand close but not touching his soft-looking white with brown feathers on his chest. Archimedes took a step down my arm and touched his chest to my fingers. He was so soft. I moved my hand as Sean had done and Archimedes moved around so I could pet where he wanted. He was almost like a cat. I was spellbound. I couldn't take my eyes off him. Sean said something softly and I missed it, so I looked up and he was smiling. He repeated that Archimedes seemed to have made a new friend.

Sean stepped away and I started to panic. He said he was just going to just get him some treats and that I would be fine. I looked back at Archimedes and he looked just as shocked as I did. It made me laugh. I went back to stroking his feathers and he made chattering noises like he was talking to me. Sean mentioned, as he walked back in the enclosure, that Archimedes was a talker and that it was okay if I moved around, just to keep my arm steady and my movements fluid. If Archimedes lost his balance on my arm I may end up with a wing in my face.

He walked over and set a bit of raw meat, chicken, I think, on a glove of his own and Archimedes spread his wings and gently hopped over to Sean's glove. I hadn't realized how light he actually was until he hopped off. I think I finally took my first breath after entering the enclosure. Sean said he only weighed about sixteen ounces, about the weight of a small bottle of water, but what he doesn't have in weight he makes up for in strength. Archimedes finished his treats and then fluffed out his wings. Sean asked me to hold out my arm again and Archimedes took flight, circled low inside the enclosure and landed back on my arm, nudging me with his head to resume the attention.

Sean came over with a bit of leather and fixed it to Archimedes' leg. He put the ends in my glove and told me to hold them lightly. He said if Archimedes felt like he was going to fly, to let go. He would stay close and Sean could call him back if he strayed too far. I looked at him wide-eyed and asked what we were going to do. He said that we could take Archimedes around while I saw the rest of the birds. Archimedes nestled into the crock of my arm and was happy as long as I was almost cuddling him. Sean laughed and said that he was a great bird but was only this friendly to the staff who had been here a while.

I looked at Archimedes and smiled, continuing my cuddle session. We wandered the rest of the enclosures and I tried to remember the names of the other birds, but it was very hard when Archimedes was vying for my attention. Sean asked for my phone and snapped a few photos of us. He sent a few to himself then handed it back. I'd have to send a couple to my mom and sister tonight. They won't believe it! Sean made his rounds and I followed with my new friend.

We checked on all the birds, Sean was holding my hand again and then we went into the lobby to visit with George. He smiled as we walked in together. George whistled lightly and Archimedes stopped cuddling with me and looked over. George whistled again and held up some chicken bits. Archimedes reluctantly took flight and landed on the perch on the desk. George laughed and said

I had found quite the friend. George stroked the owl's head and pointed to some paperwork for Sean to look over. George asked me if I'd called him back to my glove yet. I told him I hadn't but I would give it a try. My whistle wasn't the right sound, but when Archimedes was done with his chicken bits, he landed lightly on my glove and resumed his position for maximum cuddles. He was the strangest cat I'd ever held. I watched Sean make some notes and hand the paperwork back to George. Sean told George he would be back in a few hours and he motioned for me to follow him.

    I waved goodbye and stepped outside with Sean. We walked to an open field area just off the side of the lobby. It was drizzling but not hard. He told me to see if Archimedes was interested in stretching his wings. I let go of the leather straps and lifted my arm a bit. Archimedes spread his wings and was off. He soared through the field in front of us. He looped around a few times. His head snapped to the side and he changed directions. He quickly swooped down and picked up a field mouse. I gasped. Sean took my hand and we walked a little way as Archimedes took his catch to a nearby tree to eat. He smiled and mentioned that I used to work on a farm and that I should be used to things like that. I explained that I just wasn't expecting it and that it was magnificent. I felt bad for the little mouse but the way Archimedes flew through the air was beautiful. Sean smiled at me and we walked for a little bit around the field.

Sean asked if I had plans for lunch. I told him I had packed some snacks but that eating hadn't even crossed my mind. He mentioned that I had wanted to see the inside of Ashford and that they had a few nice places to eat. He asked me if I would have lunch with him. He thought he could get a table in the Drawing Room. With butterflies in my stomach, I didn't know what to say. I just stared. He started backtracking saying we can try some other time. I reached over, touched his arm and smiled at him. I told him I would love to have lunch with him in the Drawing Room. He smiled and reached into his pocket for his phone. He dialed, and while never breaking eye contact, spoke to one of the staff and arranged our table.

He hung up the phone and softly whistled for Archimedes. I put my arm out like it was the most natural thing in the world and caught him as he landed gently on my arm. His beak and some feathers had blood on them, and his feet still had a bit of the mouse. I tried not to be squeamish, so I gently stroked the feathers on his chest around the blood as we walked him back to his enclosure and tried not to look. Sean opened the door and I stepped inside. I gave him one last good head scratch, told him I would be back to visit when I could and then lifted my arm. He flew off to his perch and was content to finish his meal. Sean made a note on the board that he had eaten today and he took my glove back to put it away. We walked over to the bathroom so the two of us could clean up a bit before lunch.

9

We drove to the castle on the golf cart. Sean smiled and introduced me to the staff inside. Luke, one of the doormen, was passing by, dressed in his top hat and tails uniform. He gave me his arm and walked me inside. Sean, with a smirk on his face, followed behind. Luke gave a small tour on our way to the front lobby area and made sure I had my bearings before he showed us to the Drawing Room. Luke tapped his hat and said to let him know if we ever needed anything. He gave me a wink and shook Sean's hand before he introduced us to Sofie and returned to the lobby. Sofie, also in uniform but less formal than Luke, showed us to our seats with a bright smile. The Drawing Room was a grand room that sat at the back of the castle. It had gorgeous light blue and cream tapestry walls and furnishings. There were large windows that faced the River Corrib and a massive and beautifully manicured lawn with a huge fountain that sparkled in the sunlight when it peeked through the clouds.

We ordered a glass of wine each and the charcuterie board to start and then finished off with soup. Sean had the chicken noodle and I chose the tomato bisque. As we ate and talked, our hands intertwined on the table's edge. Not wanting to spoil things but feeling very confused, I asked him about it. He shrugged and continued to weave soft circles on my wrist. He asked me if I liked it. I said yes. He asked if I had anyone at home waiting for me. I said no. He said something in Gaelic and I raised an eyebrow.

He smiled, shook his head, and said, "It doesn't have to be complicated. I enjoy spending time with you, and I hope that you like spending time with me?" I said that I did, but that I would have to go home in five months and then what? He told me that we would cross that bridge when we came to it and said we should just enjoy it for now. I had reservations but I set them aside, for now. We would have to talk later down the road, and hopefully, part as friends. He smiled and nodded his head once like everything was settled. I smiled and told myself not to overthink it. Yet.

We ordered tea and enjoyed the rest of our meal. We talked about the next few weeks. His parents would leave for Naples next week and I'd have the shop to run all by myself. I wouldn't have another day off until they returned, two weeks later. He said he was waiting on his schedule, but it didn't change much. He asked if he could see me in the evenings after I closed the shop. I agreed just as the check arrived at the table. He filled in his employee information and told me they would add it to his tab. When his paycheck came, they just pulled it out before they deposited his check.

We walked out of the restaurant hand in hand to the smiles of the staff we passed. He asked where I was off to next. I told him Guinness Tower was my only destination and that the day turned into more than I could have hoped for. It was wonderful. He told me he had a few appointments for hawk walks that afternoon and evening, but that he would love to see me tonight. I agreed and told him to text me when he was done and we could find a place to meet.

I walked him out the door, where we parked the cart, and he kissed my hand. I flushed with what I was sure was bright red. He smiled and softly said how he liked that he could get me to blush. I smiled at him and we said our goodbyes. Just before he pulled away, he told me that Ashford had a library and that if I went in and asked for Shelly, she would show me where it was. He said I couldn't take any of the books away but that I could stay all day and read anything there that wasn't wrapped in a white cloth. Those were currently being cleaned or treated. My excitement surged through me and I fell towards him for a hug. He caught me and hugged me back with a chuckle saying how he thought that might be something I would like.

I waved as he left and turned around to head inside the castle once more. I looked around, wondering how I missed all that was around me as we came through the first time. It was beautiful inside. Exactly as I imagined it. I rounded a corner and passed a full suit of armor shining brilliantly under the lights in the hallway. The wood was a deep brown and everything gleamed in the lights. I asked the first staff member I came across where I might find Shelly and they pointed me down the hall. I made my way past some rooms with open doors and some closed. Each room I could see into was beautiful and ornate in its design and decor. I passed three more closed doors and stopped dead in my tracks. Inside the next doorway, I saw a room full of books! It had to be the library. I peeked inside and a brunette was sitting behind a little desk near the door. There was a small lamp on the desk and she had a headband on with a magnifying glass attached to it. She was restoring or cleaning a really old book in a book stand on the desk. I gasped as I walked in, there were so many books. The woman looked up with a smile.

She greeted me, "You must be Jayne." I smiled and apologized for disturbing her. I asked if she was Shelly. She nodded and said Sean had texted her. She welcomed me to the Ashford Library. Shelly explained that she was the librarian and book restoring was one of her jobs there at the castle. She gave me a quick tour with the efficiency of a well-versed librarian, told me they closed the library at five, she winked and then let me loose, recognizing a kindred book lover.

10

At first, I browsed the shelves in awe, taking in the smells and as many of the bindings as I could read. There were a couple of small tables with soft light lamps near the front of the library. Towards the back of the room, there was a couch and a couple of comfy chairs. The whole room had soft light throughout and only a few small windows on the upper floor. There were sliding ladders to help people get to the top shelves of the outer bookcases and there were a couple of step stools for the top shelves on the stand-alone bookshelves throughout the room. It wasn't the library from Beauty and the Beast, but for a private collection, I was impressed.

I had set down my backpack near one of the comfy chairs. There was a small TV tray-style desk in the corner. I set that up near the chair and went to see Shelly. I asked if she had another book stand. She smiled, reached behind her desk and handed me an X-shaped stand made out of plexiglass and a pair of white cotton gloves. I went back and set up the stand. Then I selected one of the first small books that jumped at me from the shelf, "Persuasion", my favorite Austen. I set it on the stand and curled up in the chair. I put on the gloves and gingerly opened the book. It was beautiful. The book was bound in dark blue leather. A bit battered but that only added to the beauty. The pages were thin and delicate looking, they were almost pristine, with just the corners worn and yellow.

I was lost in the story. I made it through several chapters, taking care and extra time to gently turn the pages. I was in heaven. I could spend my whole life in this library just reading every page I could. It was far too soon when I heard Shelly putting away her things. I looked at my watch and realized the time. Gently, I closed the book and placed it back on the shelf. I made a note on my phone so I could remember the page I was on. Putting the little desk back where I found it, I collected the rest of my things and turned in the stand and the gloves. Shelly pointed to a small hamper near the door for the gloves. She thanked me for coming in and told me I was welcome anytime. I smiled, thanked her for sharing all the treasures she keeps and thought to myself that I would be back as soon as I could.

I found my way out the front of the castle and headed back to The Turning Page. I wandered the path through the forest and daydreamed about the library and Sean. It was very thoughtful of him to arrange that for me. It was such a good day. And now I needed to clean up and change before he called me.

I was back in Cong before I knew it. I walked into the shop and greeted Maeve and Tom. Maeve asked how my day was and I told her about the tower, Archimedes, lunch with Sean, and the library. The day was truly magical. I told her that Sean and I were going out for the evening later but we had no plan yet so I would let her know if I would be here for dinner when I heard from him. She had a silly grin on her face but didn't say anything. I told her I needed to freshen up and change before he called so I would be down in a little bit.

    I headed up the staircase and dropped my bag in the kitchen. I cleaned out the food in my bag and what was left of Millie's apple. Then I took everything else upstairs so I could shower and change. I didn't want to go with wet hair, so I left it braided and covered it with a towel while I showered. I threw on a thin but pretty, gray sweater that I bought from a shop down the road, a new pair of jeans and my black ballet flats. I took my braids out and shook out my hair. I could work with this. I pinned the sides of my hair back, leaving the waves from the braids, and gave it a little hairspray. I put some makeup on and swiped the mascara on my lashes. I told myself twice to stop fussing but it didn't help. Just as I walked out of the bathroom to check my phone for the time, I received a text from Sean. He had gone home and changed and was ready if I was. I sent back that I was at the bookstore and I was ready when he was. I asked if he wanted to stay to eat dinner with his parents before we went out so I could let Maeve know. He sent a text saying he was on his way and that he made dinner reservations just outside of town for the two of us. I sent him a happy face and went down to the kitchen to tell Maeve.

11

As I walked down the stairs, Tom looked up from the first floor and whistled. Maeve smacked him on the arm on her way by, told him to close up and smiled at me. She told me I looked lovely and said she would package up dinner for me for lunches this week if I liked and asked when Sean was coming to get me. I told her he was on his way and that he made dinner reservations. She smiled and joined me on the first floor in the kitchen. She poured each of us a small glass of wine and sat at the table. I sat down with her and she started giving me dating advice like it wasn't her son that was coming to get me. I smiled, knowing she meant well, and sipped my wine.

Sean walked into the store, gave his dad a hug, came upstairs, kissed his mom, and produced two small bouquets of flowers, one for each of us. Maeve batted at him but was as delighted as I was. She took her flowers and mine and found two vases. She walked hers into her bedroom and said she would take mine upstairs for me. I smiled and thanked her. We said our good nights, I checked for my phone, hot spot, and my wallet, then Sean escorted me down the stairs and out to his lorry. As I stepped into the truck, he told me I looked beautiful, shut my door for me and came around. He started the engine and reached for my hand. His hands were always so warm.

We drove out of town and took a right at a crossroads. Then we drove down a long and very narrow road. I asked where we were going. All he would say was that I would have to wait and see. I asked if the restaurant had a name. He smiled and gave me a look that told me all the answers to my questions would be the same. I resigned myself to be patient and moved on to questions about his hawk walks that afternoon and the conversation flowed.

We pulled into a parking lot near a marina. I didn't see a restaurant. I saw several boats at a dock in front of us. He got out of the lorry. He opened my door and offered his hand. I got out and looked at him with a raised eyebrow. He smiled, said, "Trust me," and reached into the bed of his truck. He handed me a blanket and then put a jacket over my shoulders. It smelled like him. Then he grabbed another jacket and a large bag.

As we walked to the boats, he said he called a friend, and in exchange for bringing him dinner, we were allowed aboard and could have dinner while they tested the boat. The company his friend worked for did river cruises during the summer and they were getting the boats ready so they could open early if everything was in working order. The boats took trips and did tours of the river and Lough Corrib from Galway to Cong. Tonight, we would just be staying by the castle.

I asked what we were having for dinner and what we brought his friend. Sean said, grinning, he picked up food from George V at Ashford. They had a nice steak and potato main that his friend enjoyed, and he asked the chef to surprise us so he didn't know what we were having. I smiled back. It was a good thing I wasn't a picky eater.

We walked up to the second boat. The lights were on inside. Sean gave a loud whistle, and someone responded with a deep and raspy, "You finally made it with me steak, I see. It best still be warm." I smiled at Sean as he told his friend yes and to be nice. His friend noticed me and came down off the upper level of the boat. He pulled his hat off and offered his hand. Sean did the introductions. His name was Seamus. He was an older, salty man with windswept white hair that was long, thin and fell in his eyes. His skin was weathered and leathery and he had dark stormy eyes that held all sorts of mischief. Seamus helped me onto the boat and pointed to the indoor cabin. He said that Sean and I would be eating in there. It was drafty but the heat should be on. I walked inside. It was a little warmer, but once we started to move, I could see how there might be drafty areas. There was a small table and two chairs towards the front of the boat. There were other tables and chairs, but they were folded up and strapped to padded seats that ran the length of both sides. Seamus said he would be upstairs in the captain's cabin, but if we needed anything, to just ask him. Sean set the bag on the table and pulled out Seamus's meal. Seamus winked at me and nodded once to

Sean. As he walked away excited for his steak, he said we would be shoving off in about ten minutes.

Sean pulled out my chair and I placed the blanket on the seat then sat down. I took his jacket off for now and dropped it over the back of the chair. He did the same with the jacket he was wearing and sat. He set the bag on the floor and set the table. I was shocked. Did the chef send actual plates and silverware? Sean saw my face and said he couldn't have me eating off paper plates for our first real date. The table had a mat on it that kept everything from sliding. He opened a bottle of red wine and set it on the table to breathe, then he brought out the food and made our plates. It smelled delicious.

We started with a mushroom-stuffed ravioli with a dark and meaty demi glaze sauce as an appetizer. He poured the wine, a very dark red. Then there was a dark green salad with beets and pecans. The main was a pretty fancy steak with potatoes and early spring veggies. Everything was exceptional. We took our time getting through the meal, talking about work and family. All while watching the shoreline go by. It was twilight so the rich colors of the sunset were fading and night was setting in. We came around a bend and I almost dropped my fork. Lit up like a Christmas tree in all her glory was Ashford Castle. It was breathtaking. Everything about it screamed majestic. Sean reached across the table, touched my chin, and lightly chuckled. I snapped out of it, closed my mouth, and set down my fork. I got up from the table and went to the window. Sean got up and stood right behind me. He put his hands on my shoulders and whispered that he thought I would like this. I turned around as he put his arms around me and looked up at him. We leaned in and I closed my eyes.

Just then, Captain Seamus came over the intercom to let us know he was going to be turning around now. I jumped and Sean let me go, cursing under his breath. I walked back to the table, grabbed my wine glass, and finished off my wine. Sean called my name. I looked up. His eyes were soft and could only be described as bedroom eyes and he had a very sexy smirk on his face. I tried to change the subject by saying I had forgotten to thank him for sending me to the library today. He walked slowly over to me and softly murmured something in Gaelic. I swallowed hard, he reached out and gently took a hold of my face. He dropped his face and paused, his eyes asking permission. I nodded slightly once and he stepped forward, pressing his lips to mine. I could have stayed there forever, lost in his kiss. He wrapped his arms around my waist, I took his cap off and I ran my fingers through the back of his hair. He deepened the kiss. It was exquisite. I warmed from my core to the tips of my fingers and toes. He eventually softened the kiss and pulled back a bit, not letting go. We swayed slightly with the boat. He whispered that he had wanted to do that since the day he met me in the stables. My heart fluttered and I blushed, remembering that he had caught me from falling.

He pulled out my chair and I sat down, slightly disoriented. He took my hand as he rounded the table and took his seat. We finished our meal, still holding hands, and then cleaned up the table. He moved the chairs and the table to the side of the room and took out his phone. He pressed a few buttons and a soft song came on with a female voice singing in Gaelic. He put it in his back pocket and picked up the jackets and blanket. He asked if I wanted to step outside on the front of the boat. I agreed and he held up the jacket for me. Then he put his on. We stepped out the little door to the front of the boat and the crisp wind swiped at us. I grabbed ahold of my hair and secured it with a hair band that was always on my wrist. We stepped to the very front of the boat and I shivered. Sean wrapped his arms around me and held me steady. The music played and the boat swayed. The moon wasn't quite full, but it shone brightly on the water. He kissed my ear and the top of my head.

  We watched as the dock got closer. Soon, Seamus called down. He told Sean, "Let the pretty one stand on her own and toss the fenders out over the edge." I smiled up at Seamus and could see him tap his hat brim. Sean mumbled something about being lucky that he was a friend and old then went to take care of his request. We pulled into the dock and Sean jumped out to secure the boat to it. I went inside and picked up the blanket and the bag and went back out the side door. Seamus opened the door for me and asked if I had a good time. I thanked him and kissed his cheek. He told me, with a wink, to come back anytime and I could leave the boy at home. Sean chimed in with his thoughts on the matter and I interrupted with a smile and an, "I'll see what I can do." Sean reached over the edge of the boat, shook Seamus's hand, asked if the steak was good, and thanked him for the ride. I handed him the bag and Seamus and Sean both helped me onto the dock.

We waved our goodbyes and headed back to the lorry. Sean opened my door just as I yawned. So many things happened today and I had been up for a long time. Sean smiled and got in. He said that we should probably end the night there so he wouldn't screw it up. I agreed and scooted over to the center seat. He put an arm over my shoulder and we drove back to Cong. He pulled up in front of The Turning Page and walked around to open my door. He unlocked the door to the shop and let me in. I invited him in for some tea but he didn't want to wake his parents, so he leaned in and kissed me goodnight. My body reacted by warming from the center again. It felt nice. I started to take off his jacket but he said I could keep it until he saw me again. I raised an eyebrow. He smiled and reminded me that I said he could see me after the shop closes next week. I smiled and nodded my head. He kissed me lightly on the nose and shooed me in so he could lock the door. I waved through the window as he left and headed upstairs.

I was beat but Sam would freak out when I told her about today. I figured it best to tell her tomorrow evening so she didn't wake up Tom and Maeve. I placed Sean's jacket over the chair in my room and put on my pajamas. I saw the vase of flowers on the desk. Wildflowers, they smelled wonderful. I smiled and set my phone on the desk, plugged it in, crawled into bed and fell fast asleep.

12

The next morning the alarm went off. I shot up out of bed. I looked around and saw Sean's jacket and the flowers. *All of that, it actually happened!* I couldn't believe it. Dread set in. *What am I going to do? Long distance relationships never work! What happens when I have to go back to California? What am I thinking? Oh man, his kisses! Will they all feel like that? Wait... what do I say to Maeve? I just made out with her son! So, what if he's thirty! Oh man. I just made this so awkward!*

My mind raced the whole time I was in the shower. I got dressed and went down to the store, hoping they weren't in the kitchen and I could busy myself in the shop before they got up. Hoping didn't work. They were both in the kitchen, ready for the day and having tea. I could smell the scones in the oven. Tom looked up from his paper, said good morning and gave me a cheesy smile. Maeve had a soft smile that she tried to hide behind her teacup. She softly asked if I had a good time last night. I smiled and said I did.

She said forcefully in Tom's direction, "Good. That's all we need to know about it." He dropped his paper, put both hands up and agreed that there would be no further discussion. He smiled and winked at me when she wasn't looking. I smiled, took a deep breath and asked how yesterday was in the shop. The conversation turned towards the shop and their upcoming holiday and the tension disappeared.

Today would be a busy day in the store. Maeve over-ordered a few things to keep me stocked for the store and the fridge in the kitchen while they were gone. I would only need to go grocery shopping once while they were gone. She was so prepared. Tom and I would be organizing the new stock in the back room for the morning. We managed to make it through all the boxes with only a small comment or two about Sean and one cardboard paper cut for Tom who said it was a bit of instant karma for the comments. It actually made me feel better about dating my employer's son, that they were so relaxed about it.

Midday, Arthur and Phyllis came in for their weekly visit. I greeted them and then took over wheelchair duties. I pushed Phyllis around the store. She had come in today, not just for herself, but one of her nurses was going to be a first-time grandmother, so she wanted to get the baby a couple of books. We went to the children's section first. Finding a few more than two books, we brought them all to the register. Maeve helped us narrow down the stack to five books that were "must haves" for the new baby boy. Phyllis and Arthur paid for their items as Phyllis snuck me a candy from her pocket. She was so cute, not wanting to get caught. I smiled, pretending I was making sure no one saw me unwrap it and slipped the lemon drop into my mouth. Maeve handed Arthur the bag and I waved goodbye while I gathered the unwanted books from the counter. As I put them away, Sean sent me a text to see how my day was and to tell me he would come over to have dinner tomorrow night with me and his parents before they left on holiday. I smiled, thankful that, other than the few small comments to keep things light, things weren't too awkward. I told Maeve and she started to fuss again; she made a new list for what she planned to make for dinner tomorrow. I left her to her fussing and went to arrange a new display of bookmarks with Ireland, Cong, and The Quiet Man scenes. *I wonder where she found all these things.*

The Armstrong's made an appearance and I headed to the back the minute I saw them pass the window. I brought out their items and the latest romance novel that Maeve ordered knowing I could get Katherine to buy it. She looked at it delighted. It was the first of the series. She told me that if she liked it, she would have me preorder the next book for her.

We made our way through the rest of the day peacefully, prepping and cleaning the store. Finally, Maeve headed upstairs to start dinner as I finished placing a special order for a customer on the phone. Tom finished closing the shop and started the register close out procedures. When I finished, I headed up to see if I could help with dinner. Maeve handed me some carrots and a potato peeler. She prepped the chicken to roast and I peeled the carrots and potatoes.

As we worked, she said, "Sean is a good man. I hope you two can work something out after you have to go home." *So, she was worried too.* I told her I hoped so too and that I would never want to hurt him. She smiled slightly with a soft sigh and told me not to listen to her. That we were both adults and she was sure we knew what we were doing. I asked myself, *"Do we?"* I heard her say quietly that she's not seen him look at someone the way he looked at me and I smiled inside but busied myself with the veggies, trying to hide my blush.

We got dinner in the oven and opened a bottle of wine. Tom came up just as the cork popped. He had great timing. We sat at the table and talked about their trip. Maeve was very excited. They hadn't been to Naples yet and she was most excited to see Mount Vesuvius and Pompeii. There were museums, catacombs, ruins, castles, and cathedrals all on her list. Tom rolled his eyes at her lists but you could tell he was excited too. He mentioned being interested in taking a boat to the island of Capri. I don't know how they would fit it all in.

I got a text from Sean. He wouldn't be able to come see me tonight. One of the horses, Myrtle, had gotten sick and the vet was on his way out. Sean volunteered to stay. He wasn't sure how long it would take. I texted him that it wasn't a problem, to take care of her and to let me know how she was doing. I told him that I would see him tomorrow at dinner. We ate dinner and I sent the two of them off to take a walk while I started the dishes and cleaned up the kitchen. I finished up the last wipe down of the counters and I headed upstairs and changed for bed. It had been a very long couple of days. I called my mom and let her know I was alive. We talked for a bit and I told her about the tower and Archimedes. I left out all the Sean stuff. It would only make her worry that I wouldn't come home. She and the animals were doing well. They had been having some rain, which was always needed in California, but it made a mess in the backyard with all the animals. I let her gossip a bit since I hadn't talked to her in a couple of days. She told me about her friends and what they'd been up to and then told me about the neighbor she couldn't stand.

I could tell mom had more. I asked her if everything was okay. She just about burst and told me about Sam and Jake. Jake hadn't asked Sam yet, but he came over yesterday and asked permission to marry Sam. I thought to myself; *Sam is way too young to get married*, but then I remembered that she was twenty-three and not the six-year-old I thought of first when I thought of her. Mom asked what I was thinking but then told me that Jake didn't want to get married for a few years, but if they were going to move in together, he wanted to make things official. I relaxed a bit and imagined their wedding in a few years. It was going to be beautiful. Mom reminded me not to say anything to my sister when I talked to her and we said our goodnight/mornings.

I sent Sam a text to see if she could talk and she texted back "two minutes". In precisely twenty-three minutes she called me via video-chat. I had just enough time to sort my clothes and take them down to the small closet in the kitchen where the hidden washer and dryer were and throw in a load.

The first thing she asked was if my neighbor, Mrs. Cooper, had called me. I asked her why but she said that there was no reason. Skeptical, I asked why again. Sam sighed and explained that Mrs. Cooper may or may not have seen her carrying Lucy out of the apartment the other day. I shook my head and asked her why she just couldn't follow the rules. She explained to me, like it was the most rational explanation, that she was Lucy's emotional support person and she drove Mom nuts when Sam wasn't home at night. I told her that if I got a bill from the landlord she was paying it. She promised to keep Lucy at Mom's from now on. Then she let slip that it was better if Lucy stayed at Mom's because she liked to claw my couch, but it wasn't bad. Jake said he could fix it. I asked her if there was anything else I should know about. She quickly said no and asked how I was.

I sighed, knowing that the conversation wasn't over, but I resigned myself to find out more later and I started to fill her in on my day yesterday. She interrupted and told me to wait while she got snacks. I rolled my eyes but I liked her enthusiasm. She curled up on my now clawed up couch, set her snacks around her and told me I could begin.

I told her everything. She gasped at all the right places and swooned when it was appropriate. She could be a brat but she really was a great listener. I wasn't actually sure if she was more excited for me about kissing Sean or flying Archimedes. She asked the same question I'd been asking myself. What happens when I come home? I told her what Sean had said and she asked if that would work for me, knowing me so well. I told her I didn't know but I suppose I would find out when the time came. Though I didn't think I would be able to keep myself away from him for the next five months. I liked the way it felt when I was with him. He was very warm. He was thoughtful and pretty romantic. She asked how weird it was since I lived with his parents. I explained my morning and she was kind of shocked that it wasn't more awkward. I told her I was just relieved but I would find out how awkward it would get tomorrow night at dinner. She wished me luck just as Jake got back to my apartment with lunch for them. He asked if Sam was even still hungry after her snacks. She laughed and said it was girl talk and she could always wrap up half of what he brought her for later. I waved goodbye to both of them and let them get to their food.

    I headed downstairs with my book to finish my laundry. I poured a glass of Jameson and added some ginger ale I found in the fridge. Once the laundry was switched, I threw in my second load and sat at the table and read my book.

    Tom and Maeve came home a little while later. Apparently, their walk ended at the pub. They were a bit tipsy but made their way to the table with ease. Tom told me I should have come to the pub. I laughed and said maybe next time I would get the invite. He smiled sheepishly and then laughed, saying he bet that would have helped. Maeve examined her kitchen when she thought I wasn't looking and nodded her head once. She told Tom that she was headed to bed. He said he would join her and they left me to do my laundry and read my book.

It didn't take long to finish up my laundry and I carried everything back upstairs. I decided to run a bath since my book was at a good part. I prepped the bath and grabbed new, warm from the dryer, pajamas and headed to the bathroom. I stepped in the water and got myself settled. Just as I picked up my book, I got a text from Sean. Myrtle was going to be fine but she would need medicine for a few weeks. I was relieved for him. He said he was spending the night at the stables to keep an eye on her but would be off early tomorrow. I texted him back that I was happy that Myrtle was going to be okay but sorry he had to stay overnight. He sent a picture of his bed. It was a stall with new straw and some blankets right across from Myrtle's stall. He asked if I cared to join him and I sent him a picture of my toes in the bath water and told him that I liked my accommodations at the moment. He texted me that he was jealous but to enjoy my bath and he would see me tomorrow. I texted him to sleep sweet.

I added hot water to the tub once to reheat it, and when it started to get cool again, I figured it was time to get out, also because I almost fell asleep in the tub and could have dropped my book in the water. I dried off and put on some lotion, sealing in the warmth. Then I put on my pajamas and practically fell into bed. I turned the light off and was out.

13

The next day went quickly. The shop hadn't been too busy and we got everything ready for their time away. Sean showed up at about two o'clock. He helped his dad get all the boxes out to the dumpster and we cleaned up the back room. Sean went upstairs to take a nap in my bed for a couple of hours while we waited for closing and Maeve worked on dinner. Once Tom and I closed the store and made the deposit, we went up to the kitchen. I helped Maeve set the table and then I went up to wake Sean. He was dead asleep, softly snoring. I watched him sleep like a stalker long enough to realize what I was doing then went to the side of the bed. I wondered how he would wake up. Would he wake up slowly and just stretch or would it be like waking up Sam? When she woke up, she jumped up ready to fight. Should I stand back like I do with her? I prepared myself to catch his hands just in case but leaned in and gently kissed his lips. I warmed immediately. He slowly reached his hands around me and deepened the kiss. I broke away long enough to say dinner was ready and he mumbled that he was starting with dessert. I smiled and kissed him again but pulled away slightly. Maeve was waiting. He tried his best to pout, though he wasn't very good at it. I mentioned the pot roast in the slow cooker and he smiled and stretched. I wasn't ready when he scooped me up and I squeaked. He spun me around and kissed me again. I'm not sure I will ever get used to that feeling.

He said, "Let's go get food so we can get back to dessert." And tried to carry me down the stairs. I managed to squirm my way out of his hold and made my own way down the stairs quickly, slowing just before I was seen by his parents.

Dinner was entertaining. Maeve and Tom took turns telling embarrassing stories about Sean. He took it in stride and added to the stories when he felt the details weren't quite right. He also offered justifications for most of his actions, even from stories back when he was a very stubborn child. I shared a few stories from my childhood too. Maeve said she always thought she would have more, but after Sean, she decided he would be best as an only child. Sean winked at me. I rolled my eyes and shook my head. I was an only child for five years and I honestly don't know what I would do without Sam. She was the exact opposite of me. She thrived on chaos and never had a plan but she was also there every time I needed her.

We finished dinner and the conversation started to die out so I offered to help with the dishes. Maeve wouldn't hear it. She shooed Sean and me out for a walk and handed Tom the dish towel. He sighed but gave me a smile and walked to the sink, resigned to his lot for the evening. Sean went upstairs and grabbed a shawl from the couch that I used for reading. He came down and wrapped it around my shoulders then escorted me out of the shop. We walked the tiny streets, enjoying the quiet night. We circled around and went out to the little bridge near the water and sat. There was a slight breeze and I scooted close to stay warm. He placed his arm around my back and I leaned in. The night felt perfect and I tried really hard to just enjoy the moment and not overthink it. Sean exhaled a heavy sigh.

He softly said, "I love this town. Even in the busiest times, you can find quiet moments." He whispered to me not to overthink this. *Does he know me so well already?* I chuckled softly and whispered back that I would feel a lot better if I knew we had a plan.

Sam was the spontaneous one. I am better with a plan. He offered a thought. What if, no matter what happened, we promised to end however far we took this as friends.

I asked, "Could it be that easy?"

He comfortingly said, "It's worth a try." He took two pennies from his pocket, handed me one, and told me to make a wish and toss it in the river. I asked if I should wish for this to end in friendship? He told me to wish for what I wanted. We both took a minute, made our wishes, I leaned in to kiss him and then we tossed our penny wishes into the River Corrib.

14

The next few days went by quickly. Maeve and Tom went shopping for their last-minute needs, packed their bags and finalized everything with me. Maeve left notes for me everywhere. They made me smile. She even premade a few meals and had them in the fridge for me to reheat.

The day they were scheduled to leave, Sean took a little time off to take them to Shannon airport. The flight wasn't scheduled to leave until seven-fifteen p.m. but they wanted to get to the airport early and have dinner. It was about an hour-and-a-half drive to Shannon. Then an almost ten-hour overnight flight. The Armstrongs came to wish them safe travels and we waved goodbye after Sean loaded the car.

They left at about four p.m. Sean would return around seven-thirty p.m. I finished the day out with only two more visitors, Phyllis and Arthur. Phyllis, who had just finished a piece of chocolate as they came through the shop door, asked me to hide the evidence. I threw away her wrappers and pushed her cheerfully to the mystery section, letting Arthur look around on his own. Phyllis was dressed in a jumper and trousers and her hair looked like she just had it done. I complimented her hair, and she confirmed my guess. Arthur took her to the salon and got her a few sweets on their way to the shop. I read her the jackets on a couple of new books we had gotten in since her last visit and she chose the one she wanted to start with because one of her nurses was going to like it too and had me save the other for her next visit. Arthur met us at the register and then the two left the shop, happy with their purchase and headed back home.

At six o'clock, I closed up the shop and dropped the deposit in the safe. Maeve had pre-made chicken pot pie for us for dinner so I pulled it out of the fridge and set it in the preheated oven. I went upstairs and changed into comfy clothes; a pair of leggings and an oversized soft sweater. I found a new book and curled up in the sitting room with a glass of wine. When Sean got back, he curled up on the couch with me and put a soccer game on TV. He called it football. The timer went off and we went down to make our plates. We carried everything upstairs and ate dinner while we finished watching the game. Sean had to work early the next day so he didn't stay too late. I walked him to the door and kissed him goodnight. *This will never get old!*

Sean and I fell easily into a pattern. We both worked during the day. He would get off and come by for the evenings. Sometimes, one of us would cook or reheat, other times we would go out to eat. Spending evenings with him was very easy. Our friendship grew along with how much I cared for him. Some evenings, after he went home, I would sit and overthink. Other nights, I would enjoy it for what it was and let the worry go. Some nights I would dream about what we could have if I didn't have to leave. Some, I dreamt of how far I could let the relationship go before I left. *Will my reasonable, responsible side let me have sex with him? Is it even smart to bring that intimacy into a relationship that is doomed in five months' time?* Not having any answers, I took each day as it came, but my answers arrived soon after.

The evening before Tom and Maeve came back. Sean picked me up a little later than normal. I asked if everything was okay at work. He said yes and that he had some errands after work that kept him. We drove just out of town and made a left. As it dawned on me that we were heading to his house, he said he made dinner for me and this was easier than transporting the food to the bookshop. I smiled. It was only the second time I had been to his house and it was the first time I had been inside.

We pulled into the driveway and Sean opened my door. We walked up to the front door. The house was bigger than I expected, painted white with dark wood trim, blue shutters, and matching front door. The yard was a balance of manicured and wild. There were houses nearby but the properties were separated by either low stone walls or tall trees.

We stepped inside and it was also not what I had expected, definitely a bachelor pad but softer somehow. The entryway was a mud room of sorts. There were jackets on hooks along a small wall with a bench for taking off muddy boots. We walked through an archway, and if you turned left, there was a hallway with a few doors, and if you turned right, you were in the dining room and kitchen, and the living room was across from that on the left.

The dining room had a dark wood, rectangular table with three chairs and an L-shaped bench in the corner. The kitchen was small but bigger than his parents' kitchen. Sean decorated in blues and whites with a few soft touches and things that screamed Maeve.

We set down our things and he gave me the tour. The living room was sparse but comfortable. He had a good size gray couch that looked comfy. A TV, tall lamp, and coffee table were the only other items.

Down the hall were four doors. The first one on the left was a bathroom that looked like Maeve decorated it but was rarely used. Then there were three bedrooms. The spare rooms were on the right. One had become his workout room. It had light gray walls, a dark gray padded mat on the floor, and there was a treadmill and some weights inside. The other was mostly empty with white walls and blue carpet. It had a small bookshelf inside, bursting with books and there were a couple of boxes and a clear plastic bin with writing on them that indicated they held different holiday decorations. The master bedroom was the last door on the left and it had an en-suite bathroom. The room was decorated in greens. Sean's bed was big and the focal point in the room with two bedside tables. The frame was dark wood against light gray walls and there were matching shelves with books and pictures along the wall above a long, matching dresser. An archway led to a bathroom on the left.

We headed back to the kitchen, and he finished prepping dinner. He had made lasagna. He poured us a glass of red wine each and we went to the living room and he turned on the TV. We curled up on the couch and waited for the timer.

We sat at the table for dinner and it was delicious. Sean was a pretty good cook. He had even bought dessert. Lemon tarts with whipped cream. I took a bit of whipped cream and touched his nose when he wasn't expecting it. Which turned into him chasing me around the kitchen trying to wipe it on my face.

He caught me and we ended up with dessert everywhere. We laughed and kissed and smashed the last tart from the counter all over each other. I licked his cheek and the game that had started out silly morphed into a deep need. I could see it in his eyes. I'm sure he could see it in mine. I wanted him. I didn't care. After one deep and intense kiss, he lifted me up off the floor. We made our way down the hall, to the bedroom. I paused in the doorway when I saw his white comforter. I suggested a shower first. He raised an eyebrow but didn't argue. We headed into the bathroom. The walk-in shower had silvery grey, white, and dark green tiles. He started the water and we started kissing again while we undressed each other.

We never pulled far enough apart to truly see each other. We managed to wash off all the lemon tart between all the kissing. There had even been some tart shell in my hair. He shut off the water and offered me a towel. I took it but barely dried off, the shower did nothing but intensify my need for him. He wrapped his towel around his waist and walked towards me. I looped my finger over the edge. I pulled gently, watching it fall. He leaned closer and I met him in a crushing kiss.

We made it to the bed and he laid me down and pressed himself on top of me, holding most of his weight above me. His blue-grey eyes searched for permission. *Am I really ready for this?* I don't think, I know. I've never wanted someone more. I nodded. He pulled away and got a condom from his bedside table. When he came back, he started kissing at my bent knee. He slowly kissed down to my center. Warmth radiated out after every kiss. I moaned softly when he found my center. I was warm and wet and had never been more ready. He took his time. I started to lose my mind. Just as I peaked, he pulled back and then buried himself inside me. I climaxed as he went in hard and deep, covering my moans with kiss after kiss. His pace slowed down to a gentle rhythm as my breathing regulated. His kisses were soft. It started to build again and I tightened around him inside me. He built our pace and I was on the edge again. We reached the peak together and his pulsing climax pushed me over the edge. We drowned in each other's gentle touch and soft kisses for what seemed like hours, curling up together. He pulled the blankets up and covered us. I drifted off to sleep.

15

The next morning, I woke up in his bed, it smelled like him, his arm draped over my waist. The details of the evening flooded back to me. I warmed from my core. I started to shift a little and he tightened his hold. I rotated in his arms to face him. His eyes were closed. I kissed him on the nose and he wrinkled it. He drew me closer and inhaled deeply. He whispered that I smelled good when I slept. I smiled. I lifted my head and glanced at the clock on the bedside table. It was still early; I was so glad. I laid my head back down and snuggled in. We had time before I had to get to the bookshop and he had to go in for work.

A little while later, I woke again, this time to my stomach rumbling. He softly chuckled and whispered that someone must be hungry. We lay in bed wrapped around each other, not wanting the evening to end. When my stomach wouldn't give up and his joined in, we decided to get up and get some breakfast. He handed me one of his t-shirts to wear. We moved around the kitchen smoothly. He started the kettle and I got out eggs and butter. He put some bread in the toaster and then came up behind me while I was making the eggs. He murmured that my hands were busy and nuzzled my neck. It was very sweet but it started to tickle so I squirmed away and told him he had a bit of a mess still to clean up, pointing at bits of lemon tart all over the counter and the floor. He wondered out loud how the kitchen got so messy and then looked at me with a devilish grin. I tried to ignore him, saying I didn't recall how the mess happened, and focused on the eggs, when suddenly he was behind me again. The eggs disappeared and I heard the stove turn off. Before I knew it, I was over his shoulder, headed down the hallway. He muttered loudly that perhaps I needed a reminder.

I giggled quietly and said, "Yes please!"

The next time we emerged from the bedroom, we didn't have much time for breakfast. I snagged a piece of cold toast from the toaster, then we dressed quickly, me doing the walk of shame, wearing the same clothes I left in. He got me back to the bookstore and I kissed him in his lorry. He said he would go get his parents and they would see me tonight about seven p.m. I waved goodbye and got myself inside the store. I had twenty minutes before I needed to open the store, so I raced upstairs, showered, and changed in a flash. I put my wet hair in a librarian bun and swiped some mascara on, so it looked like I tried. I opened the store then went up to the kitchen to start the kettle and grab a quick bite to eat before any customers arrived.

The day went smoothly, though I caught myself daydreaming about last night a few times. There were quite a few customers before noon. Molly came in for a few pregnancy books. She laughed that her dark, reddish-brown hair was up in a bun too, saying it's a hair bun kind of day. I got a lull in customers by midday, so I put up a small sign and closed the store for twenty minutes while I started dinner. I got all the veggies prepped and put them and the pot roast in the crockpot. I added my seasonings and some stock, put the lid on and set it for six hours. I started a batch of rustic bread in the stand mixer and placed it in the fridge to rest until later when I could bring it out to rise.

We only got a few customers in the afternoon so, in between, I got the bread all set for baking. It finished its last rise just after I closed the store at six p.m. I made sure I did a thorough cleaning of the shop and moved into the kitchen to make sure everything was "Maeve worthy clean". Then I went up to change for dinner.

When I returned, I opened a couple of bottles of wine to let them breathe. Then, just as I pulled the bread out of the oven, I heard a car pull up. Maeve came in first leaving the men to handle all the heavy lifting. She practically ran upstairs, engulfed me in a huge hug and laughed at the glass of wine I had ready for her, taking a large swallow. She could smell dinner and was so relieved there was food. Travel could be exhausting and something about coming home made it more so. You just couldn't wait to be home.

As the men came in with all the luggage, I noticed there was an extra suitcase. They made it upstairs with all of it and took it into the bedroom. On their return from the bedroom, I had a glass of Jameson for each of them. Tom looked at me and the glass and said, "bless you", but I'm not sure if he said it to me or the glass. Sean kissed me hard and took the glass with a smile. I told everyone I would serve if they had a seat. I served up dinner and sat with my own glass of wine. They ate in almost total silence for about fifteen minutes until Tom came up for air. He broke the silence with a deep breath and a satisfied sound. They complimented me on dinner and then we heard stories from their holiday. Sean leaned back with his glass of whiskey in one hand and my hand in his other.

    The evening passed quickly with stories of their travels. Maeve did most of the talking. They had a wonderful time, and though they were happy to be home, it may be on the list of places for them to travel to again soon. They saw a lot but also missed so much. They had a few hiccups, mostly on the way home, but I told them that I thought that was the way it should be. You are sad to be leaving but the journey home is so hectic that it makes you happy to be home and wanting to go back all at once. Maeve smiled and agreed.

    It wasn't very late and the time change wasn't bad but traveling all day zapped their energy, so Tom and Maeve went to bed early. I offered to open by myself tomorrow so they could sleep in. I got an exhausted nod from Maeve and a wink and a smile from Tom. Sean and I went for a walk so we wouldn't disturb them. It was warmer that evening but I still needed a light sweater. We walked near the river to the abbey and then out to the glass roofed prayer building. It had gotten dark but it was a full moon so we could see everything until we got deeper in the woods. It was still bright enough to see where we were going and the moon peeked through the canopy in places, illuminating the turquoise glass of the walls. It was beautiful.

Water drops fell through the canopy lightly so we sat inside the building. Some of the leaves from last fall still lay on the glass roof. Sean held me close. I refused to ruin the evening so I left my questions and concerns unsaid. I just enjoyed the time I had with him. He seemed content to enjoy the time with me. We didn't have to talk. It was just comforting to be near him, always touching.

A bit of time passed. He asked when my next day off was. I told him three days from now. He had that day off too so we made plans to go to Galway for the day. I asked if I would see him in the evenings and he said he could swing by a few nights and invited me back to his house as well. I told him we could see how things worked out. We both had silly smiles on our faces. It was getting late so he walked me back. We kissed goodnight for what seemed like hours and seconds all at once. I waved goodbye as he drove away. I headed upstairs after checking on the store and the kitchen, sank into bed, and was asleep before I knew it.

16

I woke up from a nightmare in the middle of the night. I hadn't had night terrors in a long time. The kind of dreams that felt so real that you woke up shaking. It took a few minutes to walk myself through the dream so it ended better and I tried to get back to sleep but the dream was about having to leave and the heart wrenching goodbye between Sean and I. *What was I going to do?*

Morning barely broke and I slept restlessly. I gave up trying to sleep and went down early, careful to be quiet. I put the kettle on and busied myself making cinnamon rolls. I needed to do something. I turned on the oven to preheat and let the dough rise while I showered and got ready for the day. I made a cup of tea and then rolled out the dough. I set them all in the pan and covered it and let it rise one last time. Sitting down at the table with my tea, I couldn't help but feel very heavy and it scared me. *Have I fallen too far? Do I like Sean too much? Should I push him away? Everything just feels right when we are together.* A tear ran down my cheek. A finger came out of nowhere and touched it. I jumped. Maeve was standing next to me. She placed her hand on my shoulder and softly asked if I was homesick. I tried to shake off my feelings and wiped my face. I told her no and that I was fine. She tipped her head up as though she understood.

"This will be about my Sean then," she stated knowingly, not questioning and sat down. I looked at her and asked if it was that obvious. She told me she can see the way we look at each other and sometimes she saw me look sad when I thought no one was watching. I told her I really liked him and didn't want to hurt him or myself when I couldn't stay. She patted my arm and said, "Things have a way of working themselves out. You just have to have a little faith." I told her I wished I could see a way for it to happen. She smiled and said to give it time. Then, added jokingly that I may not even like him in three months anyway and then all this worrying would be for nothing. She told me to enjoy it now and see what happened. I told her she sounded like Sean or he sounded like her.

Maeve smiled and stood up to make a cup of tea. She noticed the pan on the stove and lifted the towel that covered it.

She said, "Someone has been busy."

I told her, "Busy mind, busy hands," as a way to explain. I got up and took a look. They were about ready to bake so I turned up the oven and placed them inside. Maeve told me that Tom would be sure to get out of bed once he smelt those. I smiled and made another cup of tea since mine went cold. We sat and talked about her travels and how my time was while they were gone. I, of course, left out the part where I slept with her son, though something in her eyes told me she knew. I got up to make the frosting for the rolls just as Tom wandered out of his room, very blurry-eyed. He smiled when he saw me take the rolls out of the oven and pour some of the frosting over them while they were hot. He made his tea and pulled out plates and forks for everyone. I set the pan on the table and placed the extra frosting near Tom. His eyes sparkled as he placed cinnamon rolls on three plates and added an extra scoop of frosting to his roll. He probably would have added a scoop of frosting to his tea but Maeve took the frosting and set it on the counter, well out of his reach.

We ate quietly and Tom went for another cinnamon roll but Maeve batted his hand away. She told him if he was planning to have another then he could stay up and help me open the shop. He stopped quickly and started to argue that I had said they could have a lie-in that morning. She told him to keep his hands off the rest of the rolls until later then. I smiled and told them I would take care of the dishes and shooed them off to their room. Maeve gave me a quick hug and kissed my cheek and headed back to bed. Tom pointed to the rolls and gave me a big smile and a wink and followed Maeve. I cleaned up the kitchen, placed the pan with the rolls on the stove to keep warm and put the rest of the frosting in the fridge. I figured, if Maeve fell back to sleep, Tom would be up for his next cinnamon roll.

I went downstairs, and since I wasn't sure what else to do, I opened the shop early. I spent a bit of time staring at the morning rain as it came down in almost a mist. All of the flower boxes around each shop had bright and happy looking blooms. The streets were wet and shiny, like mirrors. The rain stuck around for most of the day and kept most of the tourists inside. It was a quiet day in the book shop. Tom wandered around, whistling and cleaning and Maeve was working on some bookkeeping. By lunch, Tom managed to sneak a third cinnamon roll and the extra frosting was gone. I offered to watch the shop while they went up for lunch. I didn't want to be around when Maeve saw what he had done. I couldn't help but listen though. She said something about not being on vacation any more and as punishment he would be making dinner and cleaning after.

Later, he told me they were worth it as he headed out to the store to go pick up groceries for dinner. I mentioned that he should pick up a bottle of wine and maybe some flowers as I glanced in Maeve's direction. He told me she wasn't really cross with him; she just liked to fuss about his diet. I told him I wouldn't be making cinnamon rolls again if it was going to get him in trouble.

He said, "Where's the fun in that?" Then he winked and headed out the door.

The rest of the day was quiet, just the Armstrongs came in for their usual browsing session. Tom came back from the store without wine or flowers but had a mischievous grin on his face as he went upstairs to start dinner. Maeve was still pretending to be cross with him. She told me while he was at the store that he had a big, sweet tooth and if she didn't keep him in check that he would make himself sick.

Maeve closed out the register and did the deposit. I cleaned up the area near the computer then went to lock the door. She spoke as I walked by, telling me not to go offer to help Tom with dinner. From behind me someone finished her sentence with, "for it is himself that deserves his punishment!" I turned around and saw Sean standing in the doorway with wine and flowers. That must be why Tom was smiling. The best way to bring Maeve out of a mood was to invite Sean over. Sean kissed me and handed me the bottles of wine, whispering that his dad had called him. I giggled and watched as he scooped up his mom in a hug and handed her the flowers. She took the flowers with glee but said it wasn't getting his father off the hook.

"Come now, Ma," Sean said, "you know he likes his sweeties and can't control himself."

She popped off with, "Which is why the rest of the cinnamon rolls will be for the two of you for your breakfast tomorrow."

We went upstairs and Maeve took her flowers to her bedroom. Tom smiled to himself. We all sat at the table with the wine and waited for dinner to be ready. Sean asked more about their trip and Maeve was delighted to tell us about their adventure again. Tom served dinner when he had it finished; chicken curry and rice. It smelled amazing. The evening passed quickly and we talked about the places to go in Galway for my next day off. They told Sean what he should show me and where to eat. I told them that I was only in Galway for a few hours the evening I arrived and ate at the Original Tea Shop off Quay Street. Maeve agreed they had great soup and the shop itself was grand. By the time we finished dinner, Maeve and Sean had the whole day planned. I felt like I should have been taking notes but Sean reassured me that he had the day worked out.

Tom started the dishes and Maeve packaged up the cinnamon rolls for Sean to take home, leaving me just one for breakfast. I think part of her bad mood had something to do with the travel blues after a good holiday. Maeve said she was heading to bed early. Tom was finishing up cleaning the kitchen when I walked Sean out. He said he would be working late tomorrow but would see me first thing the following day. I asked if he knew what I should pack for.

He smiled and said, "Pack for Ireland!" He kissed me on the nose and then on the lips. I headed back into the shop checking my watch. *I wonder what Sam is up to.* I said goodnight to Tom as I went up the spiral staircase. I sent a text to Sam to see if she had time to video chat. I was curious if my apartment was still standing.

I changed into pajamas and curled up in bed. I started reading to pass the time and Sam called about fifteen minutes later.

"How is your gorgeous redhead?" she asked. I smiled and quickly changed the subject, asking if my apartment was still standing. She confirmed it was and that they had slowly moved a few things from home to make it more theirs. She promised no animals again but I suspected she had a few in hiding. I asked how she and Jake were doing and she said they were good. She told me she thought he was hiding something and said he seemed to be planning something. She said he had been asking random questions and wanted to take her out for a fancy dinner next week. I asked her what she thought he was planning. She said she wasn't sure and that maybe he was getting her a new puppy. I laughed and told her I hoped not and that it would have to stay at Mom's until I got home if he did.

She asked how I was doing and how my week solo went. I told her it went well and that Sean had come to see me every night. She interrupted me and asked if I slept with him. I tried to deny it but she could tell from my face, I'm a terrible liar. She squealed with delight and told me to dish. She wanted all the details. I told her I wasn't going to tell her about any details except that I went to his house and we had dinner and dessert and then it was amazing, and I spent the night in his arms. She tried to dig for more and wiggled her eyebrows. I smiled but I wasn't going to delve into that with her especially since his parents could probably hear me. She squealed and swooned. Then she tried to give me made up details in hopes that I would confirm anything she said. I rolled my eyes at her and turned down my speaker phone. She backed off and said I must really like him. I told her I did but that just made it harder. She told me that she was worried about my heart but that she thought Sean and I would make it work. Then she said to enjoy it for now and worry about how to keep it going later. I gave a deep sigh and told her that Maeve said I might not like him in three months and that I shouldn't worry about it. She laughed and said she liked Maeve. Just then, Sam's alarm on her phone went off. She told me she had to get ready for her afternoon shift. I told her I loved her and to let me know when she figured out what Jake was up to. She told me she loved me back and stressed to enjoy Sean with another eyebrow wiggle. I hung up, relieved I didn't blow the engagement surprise and set down my phone. I sent my mom a text to see what she was up to. She responded back that she was out shopping with her girlfriend, Helen, so I sent her a text asking her to tell Helen, hi, and told her I was going to sleep. I sent a follow-up text that I loved her and I would talk to her in a couple of days. She sent me back a text that said Helen says, hi, back, sweet dreams, and she loved me too. I turned off my light and lay in the dark staring at the ceiling. At some point, I must have fallen asleep.

17

The sun rose slowly and the room filled with pink light from the sky outside. I slept really well and woke up feeling better. I still didn't know what to do about my feelings for Sean but I would have to deal with that when the time came. I could smell breakfast cooking and got up and dressed quickly. Just before I opened my door, I heard a large crash and Maeve's voice. Sounded like her bad mood was still there. I heard a few more loud noises as I made my way down the stairs to see if she was okay. I found her picking up the pan that had eggs. She said she was transferring them to a dish and bumped the counter. The pan moved and burned her arm then she dropped the pan. She had a red streak on her arm. I went to the fridge and grabbed the mustard. I knew it sounded silly, I told her, but my mom swore by this, and I sat her down at the table and squirted the mustard on her burn. I told her to leave it on for a few minutes until she felt the burn cooling. I handed her a paper towel to catch any drips of mustard and then cleaned up the eggs. I told her to rinse her arm and apply it once more while I started more eggs. I brought breakfast to the table, and as I sat, I saw Tom peek out of their room. He shyly asked if Maeve was still mad at him and the look she threw at him made me cringe. She told him she was angrier that he didn't come check that she was okay. She lifted her arm; it had a bright red stripe. He saw it and rushed to her, asking what happened. I explained quietly while she scolded him some more. He took a look at it and asked her if she wanted to go to the doctor. She told him she was fine, it hadn't blistered yet and that I had tended to her. I told her if it wasn't too bad of a burn then the mustard would help. The vinegar would take the sting out and because it was kept in the fridge it cooled the burn as well. Tom looked at me and smiled. He said his gran would do that but he never knew why.

After breakfast, they went and got dressed for the day. Tom helped Maeve bandage her arm and they joined me in the shop. The day was busy and we had lots of new faces come in. There were a couple of tour buses that wound their way through the streets and floods of tourists would fill the shops and restaurants in intervals. I kept the stock of bookmarks, magnets, and pins full throughout the day and helped customers with book recommendations. I noticed there was an old man outside on the bench, resting. An elderly couple walked by him.

The woman pointed to the bench and said, "Here's a seat for you to take while I'm in the shop."

He replied to her as he sat next to the old man, "Don't forget where you've set me." She smiled and said she would try not to, then turned and walked into the shop. I welcomed her in as I saw the two gentlemen strike up a conversation and waited for their wives to finish shopping. The rest of the day zoomed by so fast we didn't have time to stop for lunch.

Molly and Grant came in and so did Phyllis and Arthur. They chatted about Phyllis's health, the baby, and about the sweets Arthur had brought for Phyllis. She shared with the Campbells and with Tom and me. She said there were too many for her to eat before she had to go back home. I offered to hide the wrappers again for her and she handed them over, smiling. Molly had found a sweet romance novel and Grant took it and brought it up to the counter with a couple of books for himself. He had a true crime book and a "What to Expect, New Dad" book hiding under it. His big brown eyes had a pleading look and he gestured, telling me he didn't want Molly to know so I nodded and bagged his separately while Molly was talking with Phyllis. He walked back, finding Molly sitting on the floor in mid conversation with Phyllis while Arthur had wandered off to look for a gift for his wife, Siobhan. I rang Arthur up for the teacup he found and for Phyllis's new book and the four left the shop to continue the conversation on the benches outside.

By the time we closed up the shop, we were starving and exhausted. I offered to buy them dinner at Pat Cohan's. They accepted but argued about who would pay. I told them we could sort that out after we ate. We grabbed our sweaters, which he called jumpers, and walked down the street. Jerry smiled as we came in. He asked loudly from the bar how their trip was as he pointed to the only open table. We ordered three Guinnesses as we walked by the bar. The restaurant and bar area were packed. A few of the locals had gathered to give the tourists a great evening. It wasn't long before the music started and everyone joined in, clapping, and singing the choruses. I don't remember what I ordered and I ate it so fast I'm not sure I could tell you what it tasted like. The music played on through the evening with tourists asking for different songs. The energy in the place was buzzing. Maeve and Tom must have gotten a second wind because they were up and dancing between tables. I crept to the bar and paid Jerry for our meal and drinks. I told him I was going back to the shop, and if Tom and Maeve asked, to let them know. I didn't want to interrupt their good time.

    I stepped out into the cool evening and slowly made my way back to the bookstore. I wanted some quiet time and needed to get my things together for tomorrow. I picked up and straightened a few things on my way upstairs. After a quick shower, I set out my clothes and packed my backpack with a jumper and my raincoat. I threw my Scally Cap on the pile, set my alarm, and slid into bed. I was asleep before my head hit the pillow.

18

I slept solidly through the night and woke to my alarm, pleased with the new softer melody I chose to wake up to. Everything here just seemed to feel slower paced and quiet. The country itself was seeping into me. I stretched and enjoyed my bed for a few minutes longer. I could tell that Maeve and Tom were already up. I changed for the day and finished packing. I set my backpack next to the stairs as I walked into the kitchen. Maeve had two brown bags on the counter with Sean and Jayne written on them. It felt like I was a little girl going to school again. I smiled as I sat down at the table, waiting for my turn at the kettle. Three cups of tea, plates with scones and jam and cream all came to the table. Maeve smiled sweetly at me and took her place across from Tom. Sean came in downstairs and Maeve was up getting another cup of tea. It was on the table before Sean made it up the stairs. We all sat quietly eating our breakfast. Sean noticed the lunch bags on the counter and laughed. He told his mom that we weren't going to primary school. She said it was just a few snacks and it was her way to thank me for taking care of her yesterday morning and for buying them dinner last night.

Sean inquired about her burn and she said the mustard worked so well. She had a reddish-brown slash on her arm but there were no blisters. I told her that it would turn brown and slough off and I hoped that she wouldn't have a scar. We finished our tea and Maeve shooed us out and on our way. Sean grabbed our snack bags and peeked inside. He kissed his mom as I put my backpack over my shoulder and we headed out to his lorry.

It was just under an hour to Galway and Sean already had his hand in the snack bag before we were out of Cong. Maeve had packed fruit and granola bars, some chocolate, and mine had that cinnamon roll that I didn't eat yesterday. I laughed and offered it to Sean. He took it and devoured it. I laughed and asked if his dad had passed on the sweet tooth. He smiled with frosting on his face. I handed him a napkin and he licked what he could off before wiping his face.

The drive to Galway was very pretty. The sky was blue with a few thin white clouds. The weather changed fast here so I soaked up what I could of the sun. Sean and I talked about our days yesterday and he laughed when I told him I snuck out of the pub. He said his day went by quickly too and that he had two evening hawk walks that were trial runs. They weren't sure if they wanted to offer evening walks and which hawks to use yet, so they tried a few last night. He said the birds did well but there were pros and cons to doing it at night. Not being able to really see the birds in flight was one of the cons but that Ireland skies at twilight were a definite pro.

Galway came into view. It was a bustling town. The shops were opening and the restaurants were bringing in their kegs of beer that lined the streets. I pointed to the places I had walked and Sean nodded. He said we should start at the shore and work our way into the heart of Galway. We drove for a little bit and made our way to the coast. He took me to Blackrock Beach. We parked and walked the boardwalk. Galway Bay was beautiful. There were gray clouds in the distance as we faced the bay, but the blue skies above and behind us held promise for the morning.

We sat for a bit on a bench and watched the waves. He held my hand and we talked about the day. The sidewalks behind us were bustling with people and cars filled the roads. It was a beautiful morning. We walked towards the Circle of Life Commemorative Gardens. It was a beautiful green space with rock pathways, statues, and waterfall fountains. It was peaceful and serene. We walked hand in hand in and around the paths of the garden. He read me the signs in Gaelic that were also written in English but the sound of the words in Gaelic were beautiful. We walked towards the lake and wandered onto the bridge. There were sculptures and a fountain in the middle of the lake. The whole area was beautiful greens with bright flowers everywhere. I could still hear the ocean waves in the bay. We sat for a bit on the bridge and enjoyed each other's company, not really needing to talk. We both sighed heavily at the same time. We looked at each other and knew what the other was thinking. This was so wonderful but my time here shortened each day. Sean smiled on one side of his mouth. He kissed me deeply and stood up. Shaking his head, he offered me a hand. He told me not to think on it and we walked back to the car.

We drove for a few minutes and parked again, this time, at the hotel we were staying at for the night on the edge of town near the river. I recognized the shops from my walk when I had first arrived. We didn't check in yet, instead we skirted the city and walked along the River Corrib. Sean pointed out the different bridges as we walked. We followed the river up for a while to a fishery with a dam and a waterfall. Then we walked over to a couple of docks. Sean whistled loudly and waved as a familiar-looking boat came into dock. It was Seamus. He smiled and waved. I heard him speak but didn't know what he had said. I asked Sean and he said he didn't hear him either. Seamus busied himself with helping tourists off his boat and never looked back at us, so we made the loop and continued on our walk. The area was filled with shops. All new ones I hadn't seen yet.

We stopped at The Skeff Bar for lunch. I ordered the Skeff Toastie and he ordered the BLT. When they arrived, we traded half a sandwich each. We ordered Guinness and a shot of Jameson each. Then we toasted to "living in the now" and tucked into our meals. It was really nice to be able to enjoy the day together. When we finished our meal, we walked the shops. The streets bustled with foot traffic and the occasional bicycle. Tourists entered and exited shops. We walked through a few of them ourselves and I bought a new scarf. Sean disappeared for a little bit in a shop. I wandered around looking for him. When I found him, or should I say when he found me, he came up behind me and draped a delicate silver necklace around my neck. There was a small silver shamrock hanging from the chain. I tried to protest but he stopped me with kisses until I gave up trying to talk. Only then did he stop and smile at me. He said it was so I could remember my time here. I started to tear up and there was a sadness in his eyes but he shook his head and took my hand. We stepped outside and he wrapped me in a hug. We both signed deeply and then continued on our way.

I walked into a bookshop and Sean asked, "Haven't you had enough of books yet?" with a chuckle. I told him that I was happiest surrounded by books. I wasn't sure what it was, just a feeling I got. I told him I felt the same when I was around him. He smiled. I didn't say it out loud, but deep down, I knew it felt like home. He told me, as we walked down the row of books, that he felt the same way about me and I had to think back to make sure I didn't actually say all of that out loud. He took my hand, leaving the bookstore, and we made our way to the hotel for our overnight stay.

We gathered our things from the lorry and checked-in at the front counter. It was a large hotel by comparison to the shops near it but not as large as I had seen in California. The room was very nice. We set our things down and started to change for dinner. Sean hadn't even gotten his shirt completely off and I had my arms around him, kissing his neck. Dinner could wait. He took his shirt the rest of the way off then said it wasn't fair, so he took hold of my jumper and shirt. They were on the floor before I knew it and he was devouring me. We made our way to the bed and he started to undo my jeans. Then we looked down at our lace-up boots. With a smile and a sigh each we sorted ourselves out quickly and were under the blankets in no time.

Sean's hands were soft and gentle as he removed the final bits of clothing we had on. He kissed me on the lips then trailed his tongue down my neck to my breasts. Pausing to enjoy each one before continuing his way down my ribs. It tickled at first, but when I started to squirm, he increased his pressure and soon it was pleasure I was feeling. He moved his mouth from one hipbone to the other, trailing his tongue across my stomach. He was tantalizingly close to the warmth at my center, though he patiently teased, coming ever so close but not quite touching. I could feel his warm breath on me. One more pause and he lowered his mouth over me. Indulging slowly as he brought me to my peak. I shuddered and arched all the while he held me tight, never stopping until I was spent.

He kissed his way up my body and lay down next to me. Once I collected myself, I moved on top of him. It was my turn. I whispered something about being fair, with a grin. Taking my time and with shaky legs, I kissed every inch of his lips, neck and chest. When I got to his ribs, he tensed up but didn't squirm. I lingered a few minutes to see how long he could hold out. He reached for my hands and I accepted victory with a smile then continued down to his hips. I placed my lips around him and heard him moan. It was my turn to indulge slowly. I brought him slowly just to the edge. He tensed and I would slow even more. He would relax a little and I would increase the pressure and speed. He whispered that I was driving him crazy.

In the blink of an eye, he sat up and had me under him. He kissed my lips and then reached for his suitcase. He pulled out a strip of condoms and put one on. He paused, looking for permission. I raised my hips to meet him. He smiled and sank inside me slowly. It was exquisite. Every sensation had heightened. I could feel everything as my pulse quickened. I kissed his neck and chest. He kissed my lips and my forehead. His pace matched my heart rate. I could feel our pulses throbbing inside me. I was on the edge and so was he. His climax sent me reeling and pushed me over the edge. We pulsated together, extending our climaxes. We slowly melted into each other's arms. He lay down next to me and pulled me to his side. We lay like that for a while not speaking, just listening to each other breathe. He ran his hand through my hair.

A short time later, we got up and showered. Once we were dressed and presentable again, we headed out for dinner. He asked me what sounded good and I said seafood and a glass of wine. He held up one finger and said he knew just the place. He said he was thinking steak so Ruibin's would be perfect. It's a restaurant and wine bar, he explained, that is known for their steak and seafood. I asked if we had to drive to get there and he said it was walking distance from the hotel. I told him it sounded great and we left the hotel. We went straight across the street, about a block up and Ruibin's was on the corner. We walked in the door and were greeted by the staff.

They sat us at a beautiful dark wood table in a quiet corner. We ordered two bottles of wine, one white for me because I planned on having fish and one red for him because he wanted a steak. I chose a Sauvignon Blanc and he picked a Primitivo, both were delicious. They had a three-course meal of your choice so we each picked off that menu. I chose the soup, the fish of the day, which was halibut and the Creme Brule. He picked the salmon cakes, the rib-eye and the bread-and-butter pudding.

We talked about how things were growing up in such different places. California was wonderful but I wasn't a big fan of the heat so the sunny days were lost on me. Sean found it fascinating. He grew up his whole life expecting rain on a daily basis and couldn't imagine a true heat wave. It got warm in the summer in Ireland but there was always a cool breeze. I told him I planned on wearing sweaters all summer because it just wouldn't be warm enough if I compared it to what I was used to. I talked of my parents and the divorce and how it didn't affect me as much as Sam. I had moved out and Sam was the one still at home with Mom when Dad left. I still talked to my dad but Sam and Mom were still angry and hurt so I didn't tell them much. I was shocked when Sam and Jake got together because she was anti-men for a while.

Sean talked of growing up in a tiny town and how there wasn't any real trouble to get into as a kid, and even if there were, his parents would find out too quickly to make it any fun. He would hang out in the woods with a few of his mates and they climbed trees, or they would go to the castle and see what mischief they could find. That is when he met George for the first time. He and a couple of his friends were caught trying to light things on fire with a magnifying glass and George found them. They had to work evenings after school mucking out stalls for a month. Sean said he just never stopped going back, and eventually, it turned into an actual job. He would split his time at the bookstore and the stables, but what he really loved were the birds, so when he was seventeen, he asked about working with them and that was the end of it. Even when he took night classes at university, he still worked both places, though his parents required him less and less.

I told him about my first job being the farm and all the animals we had growing up. Then I went to look for a job to help pay my way through college and found the stationery company. I worked as a line worker for a bit but managed to make it into the main office quickly and had been there ever since. I took other jobs here and there, but they were part time and after hours. I worked at a coffee shop, at a greeting card store, and a fabric store at one point or another.

Sean asked what it was like to have a sister. He was an only child and had his parents' undivided attention which wasn't always what a teenage boy wanted. I told him that having Sam around was both wonderful and maddening at the same time. We were always similar in size for clothes so a lot of my clothes would go missing, but I couldn't ask for a better built-in friend and listener growing up. We told each other almost everything and sometimes too much. He asked if I told her about us. I told him I had but didn't tell her all the details, though she asked for them. He smiled.

All the food was amazing. The fish was so fresh. Sean said his steak was perfect. They brought our dessert out on silver trays. We finished our meal and Sean paid the check. We walked back to the hotel and stopped at the hotel bar for a night cap. I settled on herbal tea since I had just had a bottle of wine and had to work in the morning. Sean had an Irish coffee. Our bartender, Andy, was very nice. He kept the bar tidy and told stories to us and the other patrons. We made our plan to get up with time to get ready and drive to Cong. Sean had to be at work before me so we aimed to get me back to the shop about an hour and a half before I had to open.

We took our second round of drinks upstairs to our room and drank them out on the balcony. I caught a chill and we came in for the night. We changed for bed and curled up in front of the television. Before the movie was over, wandering hands became distracting. We picked up where we left off before dinner and ended the night with me curled up in Sean's arms; all our clothes were on the floor.

19

The next morning, the alarm went off and I realized I was holding Sean's hand in my sleep. I scooted over and kissed his neck just behind his ear. He let out a soft moan, turned over, curled up around me, and nuzzled my neck. I told him it was time to get up and he told me he would go in late. I laughed knowing that wasn't true and reached over to tickle him awake. He caught my hand gently and raised an eyebrow. I smiled and kissed his nose then squirmed out of bed and headed to the shower. I climbed in and invited him to join me over the sound of the water. A few minutes later, we were lathering each other up.

It's a good thing they have large water heaters in hotels. We were in there for quite a while and the water never faltered. Short on time when we finally shut the water off and finished what we had started in bed again, I ran a comb through my hair and braided it. We got dressed quickly and packed up our things. I made Sean promise to let me pay for the hotel, but when we went to check out, it had already been paid for. He smiled at me and said he didn't know who had paid for it but the lady at the counter laughed. I threw him a dirty look but shook my head, figuring it wasn't worth the fight.

We made a quick stop for takeaway tea and a scone at The Original Irish Tea Shop and then drove straight to Cong. Sean dropped me off at The Turning Page, and with a quick kiss, he was off to work. Maeve and Tom were just making breakfast when I walked upstairs to put my pack in my room. I went down to join them at the table. They asked how my trip was and if Sean had taken me to all the places they had mentioned. I filled them in on the sightseeing, the shopping, and the food. They seemed pleased and the conversation turned to the store and the day. Maeve told me that they expected the day to be busy. There were supposed to be four tour buses headed to town today. She told me they just received a box of Quiet Man merchandise and asked if I would unpack and get as much priced and out on display as possible.

Maeve got up to make some snacks for us to put in the fridge behind the register and I made myself another cup of tea. I went upstairs to dry my hair since I had time before we opened. The three of us seemed to head down to the shop at the same time. We all met at the bottom. Maeve took charge and handed out chores. We had the place sparkling and all the merchandise out before the first bus pulled into Cong.

The Armstrongs came to the shop for a browsing session early to beat the crowd. They said they had gone to the shops for groceries and planned on reading quietly and staying out of the hustle and bustle. By midday, the whole little town buzzed with excited tourists. I understood why the Armstrongs came in early. The register beeped and chimed the rest of the day. You could almost make out a melody with the chimes on the front door, the register, and Tom whistling softly.

I kept the stock moving throughout the day and handled any special orders, but mostly, it was quick buys for people who only had a few hours in town. Tom helped people find items and offer ideas for gifts and last-minute buys. Maeve manned the register and never left for a minute. We ate quickly throughout the day when we could find time.

We finally closed the shop after helping the last customer before her bus left that evening. One of the buses had an overnight stay planned so the town buzzed with people milling about in and out of shops before they closed. The restaurant and pub were packed with people waiting for tables out the door.

It was the kind of day that exhausted and excited you all at once. I sent a text to Sean to see what his plans were for the evening. He said he was just finishing up and planned to come over. I mentioned the whirlwind day and he offered to take us all out to dinner. He said he would call Cullen's at the Cottage and see if they had a table for four. When he sent me back a text telling me it was all planned out, I walked over to Maeve and Tom. They were packing up the store a bit, closing out the register and talking about a glass of wine while they figured out dinner.

Maeve was so pleased she said the rest of the cleaning could wait until tomorrow and we went up for that glass of wine and waited for Sean. He came by and picked me up. His parents followed in their car. I know I ate but I was so hungry I couldn't tell you what it was or what it tasted like. I do know the Guinness was flowing and I probably had one too many. We ate and talked for a few hours about our day and then called it a night. Tom and Maeve headed back and Sean helped me to the lorry with a smirk. He mentioned that I didn't have to finish that last pint. I told him I was hoping for a good night's sleep even if I had to do it alone. He said I didn't have to sleep alone if I didn't want to and wiggled his eyebrows like Sam does. I laughed and told him he was welcome to stay the night in the little full-size bed but he would have to learn to be quiet.

We laughed and talked on the short drive back to The Turning Page and he parked his car. When he got out it dawned on me, he wasn't kidding. *Was he planning on staying the night?* I had just enough beer in me to not overthink the awkwardness that might be there in the morning and went with it. Though I think he saw the slight panic on my face and told me not to worry and that we would just sleep tonight but he wanted to wake up with me in his arms. A warm feeling washed over me. It was probably the most romantic thing anyone had ever said to me.

We walked into the shop and locked up behind ourselves. We headed upstairs and Maeve and Tom were at the kitchen table. We said good night and I tried not to make eye contact with them. Tom told us to have a good night with a lilt in his voice that told me I would blush if I looked at him. Maeve said she would make a full Irish breakfast in the morning if Sean would be joining us. He perked up at that and said he could go in late since his first hawk walk wasn't until half-nine. I told them I would see them in the morning and wished them sweet dreams. I climbed the stairs quickly to hide any embarrassment. I tried to remember the state I had left things the last time I was in the room. Thank goodness my mother was adamant about making our beds in the morning when I was growing up.

I grabbed my pajamas from behind the pillows and put them in my hamper. I pulled out new, cuter pajamas and changed while Sean was in the bathroom. When he came out, it was my turn. I brushed my teeth, ran a brush through my hair, then braided my hair on my way to bed. Sean was waiting in bed for me. He had put on a pair of pajama pants from the small closet chest that held a few sets of clothes for him just in case he stayed the night. He held out his arms and flung the blankets back giving me room to snuggle in next to him. We settled in and he stroked my hair and quietly hummed a haunting lullaby. It wasn't long before I fell asleep.

20

The week went by about the same; Sean and I had our work during the day, and at night, he either stayed with me or I would go to his house. We spent very few nights apart. One night, I got a call at three in the morning while I was sleeping in Sean's arms. I jolted up out of bed and grabbed my phone. Sam's face was on the screen, and before I could even say hello on the video-chat, she was screaming. I panicked and asked what was wrong. The camera was bouncing all over the place and I couldn't tell what was happening. Then it dawned on me the screams were happy screams and I smiled. Jake must have proposed. Sean was trying to figure out what was going on, so I turned down the speaker a little and whispered to him what I thought it was. He relaxed back into bed. I called Sam's name a few times and then she remembered that she called me. I was right, he had proposed. She was ecstatic. I congratulated the two of them. She told me she was sorry for calling so late or early but she had to share. I told her I understood. Sean reached around my waist and pulled me close. I lay down next to him and listened to how the proposal happened. Sam finally made eye contact with the screen and noticed Sean behind me. She apologized again and told me to get some sleep and to call her tomorrow after work. I told her I would and congratulated them again. Sean and I snuggled up and fell back to sleep quickly.

I called Sam the next evening from my room after the shop closed. She was still beaming and talking really fast. Sean couldn't understand her. I laughed and told him that there was an art to understanding an overly excited Samantha Rose. He put up both hands and said he would leave me to it and went down to the kitchen. I let Sam spill all the details. She explained every minute of the evening. How she had done like I said and just went with it, how much work Jake had put into the whole evening, and how she couldn't believe it when he popped the question. Sam was at our mom's house, so mom chimed in here and there, making sure I had every detail. After an hour and a half, I think I heard the story twice all the way through. Mom and Sam had a tendency to jump around a lot when they got excited about things. I told them a little about my trip to Galway and we ended the call with my mom asking when I was coming home. Soon, was my answer. With a smile, I reassured them I would be home before they knew it and we could plan all they wanted for the wedding. I blew them both kisses, congratulated Sam again and said goodnight.

I went downstairs, so happy for Sam, but in need of a glass of something. You didn't just have conversations with my family when they got like that. You had a full-on experience. I think that phone call took more out of me than the whole day at work. I felt like I had run a marathon.

Sean smiled softly at me as I descended the stairs. He had a glass of Jameson and ginger ale in his hand and held it up for me saying he thought I might need this. I chuckled and took it with a smile. I explained that she was excited and had a lot of energy. Sean gave me a hug and said he was glad he was an only child. Maeve batted at him and announced that he would have been a grand big brother, but she wasn't willing to put up with two wee devils and that he was mischief enough for her.

Maeve was still working on dinner and Tom and Sean had started a game of cards. I kissed him on the cheek and nodded my head to his dad. He smiled, said he was happy for Sam and Jake, then went back to playing cards. I walked over to Maeve. She was just finishing dinner. I asked if there was anything I could do. She told me to get the bowls and small plates for everyone. Maeve had made chili and cornbread. I helped her serve up dinner and the four of us played cards for the evening. I told them about my conversation with Sam and my mom. I was really excited for her. The wedding, on the other hand, was going to be hard work as Sam's taste ran expensive. I told them it was a good thing they weren't planning on getting married for a few years. We would all need time to save for it.

After a couple of hours of playing cards and talking, we said our good nights and headed to our rooms. I laughed to myself and Sean heard me. He asked what was so funny and I told him I could already see both my mom and sister planning the wedding. I bet that they were sitting down right then, trying to plan the whole thing and they might just have the whole thing worked out before I got home.

21

A few days later, Maeve had a delivery. A dozen boxes showed up at the shop just before it opened. We were eating breakfast when we heard a knock. Tom went down to answer the door. He called up to Maeve, asking what she had ordered. She told him they were for the school outings this week. I looked at her quizzically. She explained that there were a few schools in the area that take a school outing to Ashford Castle and then they come to Cong to shop and have lunch, so she stocked more children's books and toys for the week.

We finished up breakfast and cleaned up the kitchen, then went down to open the boxes and set up new displays. Tom brought out a couple of round tables and some clear plastic display stackers. We set them up near the front of the store. Then he brought out a long skinny table that we put up in the children's section. We loaded the displays with new and extra books, stuffed animals, and toys.

We had things all set at about half-past-ten that morning. I wiped my forehead and asked what days the outings were scheduled. Maeve said there should be a bus or two each day this week. The schools in the area coordinated so they didn't flood the castle or the town.

A few hours later, a long yellow school bus with a white top pulled into town and unloaded. A few teachers and parents lined all the kids up, single file. Maeve waved at one of the teachers from the open front door. The teachers and parents walked the kids to Pat Cohan's first. I watched as Jerry held the door and deposited a brown lunch sack into each child's hand as they went inside for lunch.

Maeve called me to the kitchen to eat quickly before the kids finished. She explained that we were the next stop for them after they finished eating. We scarfed our sandwiches and Maeve made one for Tom. When we were finished, we prepared for the onslaught of kids in the store.

Just under a half an hour later, the teacher that Maeve waved at called out from down the street.

Maeve stepped out the door and waved, saying, "We are ready for you, Brigid." Maeve stepped back inside and told me that Brigid was Katherine and Donnie's daughter-in-law. She married Donnie Jr.

Brigid lined all the children up just outside the store and gave out a few last-minute behavior instructions before she let them come inside. I watched all the children nod in agreement and then walk quietly into the store. There were at least forty of them; as soon as they made it inside to the first table of items, they scattered into all the aisles. What started out as a lot of little eight and nine-year-old whispers quickly turned into a consistent buzz of noise with the occasional loud burst followed by a handful of shushing. Brigid had five parents with her for backup. They walked the store and kept an eye on who they could.

I walked around and helped children asking for books on upper shelves and talked with them about their toy choices. They all wore blue plaid uniforms with white polo shirts. One little girl with vibrant red, Dutch braids and freckles across her tiny nose asked me about my accent. When I told her I was from California, she told me they had learned about America in school and asked how long the flight was to get to California. I told her that it took about eleven hours, sometimes more. Her eyes opened wide with astonishment. Then she told me she wanted to visit one day but eleven hours was a very long time. I started to agree with her but a book caught her eye on the shelf. She had the stuffed animal on the front and said she had all the other books. I handed it to her, she thanked me, and she ran off with her friend to go look at the toys.

A little boy reached up and tugged on my shirt sleeve. In the sweetest Irish accent, he asked if I could reach the green dragon book on the top shelf. I looked at where he was pointing and found the book he wanted. He said, "Tanks very much!" and walked toward the register.

The children spent about an hour and a half wandering the store, while Brigid and Maeve conversed. Then Brigid became Mrs. Armstrong and blew her whistle in three short spurts. Then she announced that they had five minutes left and for anyone who was ready to get in line at the register to purchase their items. The children made their way and Mrs. Armstrong, and a couple of parents walked the line, asking each child about their purchase and how much money they had brought to spend. Some children had to make decisions and put items back and others found they had enough to add small items from around the register area.

Tom, Maeve, and I set up an assembly line at the register, while some of the parents helped the children not yet in line make decisions. I would take the items and scan them and hand them to Tom who was ready with the bag and Maeve would take the money and hand them their change. Tom would give them their purchase and Mrs Armstrong would lead each child to the line she was creating at the door.

We got through everyone quickly and waved goodbye to them as Mrs. Armstrong led them from the shop. Dozens of children waved back and held up their toys for each other to see while they slowly exited to the street. Their next stop was a sweet shop at the end of the street. I overheard Mrs. Armstrong say that she was hoping most of them spent their money at the bookshop and wouldn't be able to stock up on sweeties. I hoped, for her sake, she was right. That was going to be a very long bus ride back if they were all sugared up.

We took a deep breath in unison and then Maeve opened the little fridge behind the register. She pulled out a bottle of Prosecco and some glasses and announced she was glad she thought ahead, and it was time for a celebratory drink. It was so out of character for her but she followed her comment up with another, saying Sean was a handful, but my goodness, that was a lot of children. Tom and I made eye contact but didn't say anything and walked over to collect our drinks.

Just then, two voices came through the door. A second or two later, Donnie and Katherine walked through the door with bright smiles on their faces. Those smiles only got bigger when they saw the bottle and the glasses in our hands.

Donnie said with his mischievous smile, "It looks as though we've arrived just in time!"

"How grand!" Katherine followed. Tom handed Katherine his glass since he hadn't had any yet and walked upstairs to get more glasses. Tom came down a couple of minutes later with two short glasses with what I can only guess was Jameson. Maeve poured some more into her glass and offered more to Katherine, asking if she wanted "a bit more sparkle". Maeve explained that Brigid had come in with her class and it seemed like a couple of other classes too. Katherine laughed saying she had seen them and said hello to her and the children just before coming in. She took a sip and said it was lovely, then walked around the store, browsing with her "sparkle".

Donnie and Tom walked over to the non-fiction section with their whiskey and I took my glass over to the children's section to tidy it up. We finished out the day putting out more stock and preparing for the next bus or two tomorrow. It was going to be a busy week.

22

My next day off was a couple of weeks later. Sean had to work so I decided to spend some time in the woods with my book. I packed my backpack and headed downstairs. Maeve was done with breakfast and was getting dressed for the day. Tom was sneaking another scone. He pressed his finger to his mouth and made a shushing sound. I smiled and picked up the brown bag Maeve had set out for me and put it in my backpack. Then I made some tea in a travel mug and wrapped a scone in a napkin. Sean came down and mentioned my raincoat and an umbrella. I patted my backpack which also had my half yoga mat, a small lap blanket, and a book. He smiled at me and tipped his imaginary hat. He kissed me on the nose and told me not to get caught in a downpour.

    I went out and locked the door behind me. I wanted to explore a bit more of the forest before I stopped to read. I crossed the bridge near the old fishing house and hopped across the imaginary county line in the middle of the river. I passed by the glass building because it was so beautiful. I couldn't help but want to come by and see it whenever I came out here. As I wandered the forest, I noticed the trees seemed exceptionally green. Even the moss was bright and fluffy-looking. Ireland in the late spring and early summer only got more beautiful. Walking around in the forest near the glass building, I managed to find a spot where I could see the sunrise just below the forest branches. The bright gold rays shone through them and illuminated the forest around me. I followed one of the rays that caught my eye and walked in its light further into the forest. Up ahead, a sparkle in the sunlight caught my eye. A small pool of water surrounded by stones. With a hole in the ground just above it created by tree roots. It looked like a fairy's home. Near it was a round circle of mushrooms. *A fairy circle!* It was extraordinary, and not being terribly superstitious but still recognizing the lore, I stepped forward but not too close. I tried to recall the folklore of fairy circles. I believe that fairy circles were the result of fairies dancing, and if you crossed a fairy circle, you could get trapped and be forced to dance with them forever. Not being a great dancer and not wanting to take my chances, I watched the little pool, and took some pictures with my phone from a distance, and moved on without disturbing the area. Also, a thing to note is that most mushrooms that grow in circles like that are usually poisonous, which may explain the lore. Belief in the fae or not, I had my day planned out and dancing or dying was not on the agenda.

Making my way carefully through the forest, staying on the trails that were before me, and keeping myself oriented so I didn't get lost were my chief tasks on my walk. Not to mention, taking in all the beautiful sights and colors around me. I was heading in the direction of the castle but taking the long way it seemed. I found the bank of the river and reassessed my direction. Looking across the river, I saw the paved road leading to Ashford peeking through the trees. I thought to myself that it probably would have been easier to just take that, but I wouldn't have seen the fairy house or circle, and the forest on this side was so untouched and wild.

The forest was so active with life. I could hear the small creatures scurrying along the ground and through the trees. I could hear the birds singing. I heard an owl hoot and thought of Archimedes. I gradually made it through the forest. The smell was so fresh. I narrowly avoided a large spider web and stopped to watch the little beads of water shimmer on the delicate threads. I could hear some people in the distance hiking through the forest too. I came across a path that had horse hoof prints and guessed that this was the part of the forest Ashford equestrian center took their riders. I followed the tracks backwards and they led me straight to the equestrian center. I paused and checked my lunch bag from Maeve and there was an apple. I pulled out a small pocketknife that I had in my checked bag from California and cut a few slices for the horses.

The stables were hopping with riders and staff. Some worked on morning clean-up and others prepared horses for rides. I checked my watch for the time. The early morning got away from me in the forest. It was already nine a.m. I walked through the stables and said hi to the staff and the horses. I stayed out of the way as best as I could. Millie was very vocal about her treat. I brushed her face with my hand while she took her treat. She nudged me with her head. One of the stable hands walked up to us and asked if I was ready for my ride. I told him I hadn't scheduled a ride and that I was just visiting. I asked if I was in the way. He said I wasn't, but that Millie was up for a ride this morning. I kissed her face and gave her one last piece of apple then moved down the line. I found Cara and Colleen and made sure they each got a piece of apple too. Colleen's was just a small piece. I wasn't sure if she was ready for treats yet.

When I found myself to be more in the way than not, I decided to move on. I walked down the road and headed straight for the castle. I hadn't actually ever entered through the front door. Luke welcomed me back, mentioned it was my first time through the front doors with a mischievous smile as he opened the door for me and asked if I needed help finding my way. I declined and told him I was heading to the library to see if Shelly was there. He smiled and bowed his head a bit. The castle was amazing inside and out. Every time I came in, I was in awe. I walked down the corridor to the library. Shelly was at her desk. She heard my footsteps, even though I was trying to be quiet and looked up. She smiled when she recognized me and pulled out a book stand and gloves for me again. There was an older gentleman in the library today. He was wearing white gloves as well and I saw that he had set himself up at one of the small tables nearest the door. I went and recreated my side table and comfy chair set-up from my first visit.

I had several free hours so I picked out "Persuasion" again to finish. I sat and dove into the story where I left off. I suppose I got too lost because I finished the last page and shut the book quietly with a sad but contented sigh, then I looked at my watch. It was just past noon. I put the book back on the shelf, took off my gloves and draped them over the book stand. I grabbed my backpack and walked over to Shelly. I told her I was taking a lunch break with a smile and that I would be back for more. She smiled at me and told me she would keep an eye on anything I didn't want to have to carry around if I wanted. I thanked her but left with my backpack. I went out the little side door that Sean had brought me through on our first lunch date. There was a small gravel path that stretched around the castle and I followed it to a small wrought iron table with two chairs in the corner of the garden.

The clouds were building but the sun was peeking through, so I had a few minutes before the rain came back. I opened my lunch bag and Maeve had made me a ham sandwich and there was a bag of crisps. I pulled out my bottle of water and guzzled half the bottle. I had forgotten to drink anything today. I finished my sandwich and crisps and the rest of my water before the rain started again. I walked into the castle again and found the bar. I asked the bartender if she would mind filling up my water bottle. She smiled and reached for it, asking me to take the lid off. I thanked her and asked if there was a charge. She laughed and said no. I drank a little more and placed it in my bag and went back to the library.

I took a deep breath as I entered. I loved that smell. I decided to look for a book I had never read, one that should be read in Ireland. I asked Shelly to name a few books that anyone who came to Ireland should read. Something old, and of course, something that was in the library here. She offered "The Last September" by Elizabeth Bowen, "The Importance of Being Earnest" or "The Picture of Dorian Gray" by Oscar Wilde, and "Ulysses" by James Joyce. She paused for a moment and said I could always go with Bram Stoker's "Dracula". I thought for a moment and asked where I would find Bowen's "The Last September". I had read both the Wilde's, Joyce was a bit heavier than I wanted to get into, and "Dracula" was a classic that I had read and seen several times. She told me "The Last September" was a heavy book too but that the books written in the late 1920s were either heavy or too light, but the main characters in this book hid the seriousness by pretending it wasn't happening and having lavish tennis parties and army camp dances. I thought to myself, *pretending it's not happening... like pretending I don't have to go home in four months.*

She took the book off the shelf and went to hand it to me. I hadn't put my gloves back on, so she stopped and walked it over to my chair and placed it in the book stand for me. She asked if I needed anything else. I told her that I was good and I curled up in my chair and started to read. The theme of the book ran parallel to my life only in that I didn't want to face the big issue. That's where the similarities ended. The book was well-written and I did get immediately sucked in by the characters. I whiled away the next couple of hours with Bowen and her characters, Sir Richard Naylor and his wife, Lady Myra, completely entranced in the story. My phone buzzed with a text from Sean. He wanted to know where I ended up on my grand adventure. I told him I was at Ashford's Library and I could almost hear him laugh. He said he was done with work and asked if I was interested in a ride back. I told him I was and made my notes in my phone where I ended. I placed the book back where Shelly had taken it from and cleaned up my spot. I thanked Shelly for a great day and a great recommendation and walked out of the castle towards the falconry.

Sean met me part-way with the cart. It had started raining again as I was walking and he got to me just as I was reaching for my umbrella. We took the cart and put it away then walked to his lorry. He asked me to stay the night with him at his house tonight. I agreed and asked him to take me to the bookstore first so I could get clothes and we could have dinner with his parents. Maeve was making grilled cheese sandwiches and tomato soup.

During dinner, I told them about my walk through the woods. The superstitions flew from Tom when I got to the part about the fairy circle and the spider's web. He told me how I narrowly survived and he would have to keep a better eye on me to make sure the fairies hadn't messed with my head. We laughed and took turns with our stories of the day. During Tom's story, I paused a moment with a catch in my breath. I couldn't help but feel the sadness that rocked through me knowing I would have to leave this place and these people I had come to love. It brought tears to my eyes. I tried to hide it but I could tell Sean saw it. Maeve's voice brought me out of my own head as she shooed the two of us out and on our way for the rest of our evening. I started to gather the plates and she would hear none of it. She took them from my hands and handed them to Tom who begrudgingly took them to the sink, throwing a dish towel over his shoulder and starting the dishes. I headed upstairs with Sean to pack my bag. Lost in my own thoughts and not really thinking about what I was packing, I mechanically placed things in my backpack.

Sean gently took my hand and pulled me into a hug. He held me so tightly I couldn't help but melt a little. He pulled back and put his hands on my cheeks. I could see him resigning himself to having this conversation. He said that we could talk on the way to his house and all night if it would make me feel better. I wasn't sure it would but we needed to talk this through. He kissed me on the nose and let me go back to packing. I looked in my bag, surprised that I had done so well on autopilot. I pulled out a couple of shirts that I wouldn't wear unless I was gardening and replaced them with a sweater and a soft nightgown. Feeling okay with the rest of my choices, I headed to the bathroom for toiletries. Once everything was packed, Sean and I went downstairs to leave. I told Maeve I would see her in the morning for opening. She told me to take my time coming in. *Now I knew she saw the tears too and she knew we have a long night of discussion ahead of us.*

Sean took my bag and opened the lorry door for me. I climbed in and took my bag and placed it at my feet. I took a deep breath to calm myself as he came around to his door. I saw him do the same. I'd found serious talks seemed to go better when they happened in a vehicle. You didn't have to look into each other's eyes, and you couldn't just leave the conversation. It was quiet as we left town. I took another deep breath getting ready to begin, but Sean interrupted me. He said that the last couple of months had been amazing. He said, with earnestness glancing over at me a few times, that he did not expect to feel so much so fast and that he'd been struggling with the thought of me leaving every day. He took a shuddered breath and continued. He said he wasn't sure where this was going to go or whether it would last when I went home but that being with me felt right.

When I reached for his hand, he held on tight. I tried to be brave and told him that this story was destined to end in heartache if we kept this up. I asked if it wasn't better to end things now and not get so bound to each other, making the time when I did leave that much worse. I stressed that I was only trying not to hurt him or myself. He squeezed his eyes shut for a couple of seconds and sighed deeply. He pulled into his driveway, shut his eyes, turned off the lorry, all without letting go of my hand. He opened his piercing eyes, light blue tonight, and I could see the hurt and the sorrow, but there was more.

He lingered, holding my attention then asked, "Can you honestly tell me that you don't feel bound to me at all? Because, from the moment I saw you in the stables, I've known that I need you in my life." My heart skipped a beat, taking my breath away. His gaze would not let me look away. I started to tell him no. My head knew it was what I should have said, but my heart wouldn't let me. I stuttered and closed my mouth. I looked down. A tear fell, landing on our hands.

I whispered, "I just don't see how this is going to work." He touched my chin, bringing my eyes up to meet his again.

"I don't want you hurting but I want you in my life. If that means I have to wait until you have figured the whole thing out in your head then I will, but I am not going anywhere. I can be your friend and we can still go do things together. We can still enjoy each other's company and have dinners together just as friends, but I want you to know that I want more, and when you are ready, I will be right here to pick this back up." He pulled me close and sealed that statement with an exclamation point of a kiss. All I could think, when he was kissing me, was that I was so in love with him, and as he pulled away, despair took its place.

He asked me if I would still like to stay with him that night or if I would like him to take me home. The tears just wouldn't stop so I nodded my head and whispered, "Take me home." He nodded his head and started his lorry again. The drive back was quiet but he tried to make it light by suggesting that taking me back was probably for the best since we were just friends now and he might have had a hard time keeping his hands off me. I smiled at his playfulness but my heart was breaking and the pain was unbearable. I just wanted to be numb. He pulled up to The Turning Page and hopped out of the lorry. I opened the door, and taking my bag with me, I stepped out. He pulled me into a big hug. I hugged him back but pulled away quickly. Being in his arms just hurt my heart. He kissed me on the cheek, looked me deep in the eyes, and then let me go. I could see he wasn't as okay with this as he sounded. I stepped inside and watched him drive away. I listened and Tom and Maeve were still in the kitchen. It got quiet. I raced upstairs, not stopping to say goodnight. I dropped my things in the bedroom and headed for the shower. As the hot water hit me, the taste of my salty tears diluted. The sounds of my sobs were drowned out by the water. Eventually, I was all out of tears and the water was cold. I took my shaking body out of the tub and dried off mechanically. I put on my warmest pajamas and crawled under the covers.

 I woke in the middle of the night crying again. I hugged my pillow tight and waited for it to stop. I walked toward the bathroom to get a drink of water and noticed a note from Maeve telling me to take tomorrow off taped to the inside of my door. I got the water and brought it back to bed with me. I could feel my face was swollen and my eyes were puffy. It was only going to be worse in the morning. I resigned myself to sleep in and to take the morning to sort out what I was going to do.

I woke up around ten and my face was definitely puffy. I lay in bed and let the sadness take over. The water stains on my pillowcase told the tale of a lonely night. Needing something to do, I stripped the bed and took the sheets down to the washing machine. Maeve and Tom were downstairs in the shop with a couple of customers. Maeve had left a plate of breakfast on the stove. I picked at it but I wasn't hungry, I couldn't feel anything. I headed back upstairs and sorted out another load of laundry to do. I brought it down and traded out the loads when the first one finished. I grabbed a piece of bacon on my way back up. Searching for things to keep me busy, I cleaned our... I mean, my room and organized my things in the bathroom. Then I headed back down to switch out the laundry. I brought the sheets back up and made the bed. It was half-past-noon when I went back down for my load of laundry and I heard Maeve coming up the stairs. I rushed upstairs with my load and tried not to drop anything. Maeve saw me but blessedly didn't say anything. I folded my laundry mechanically and put everything away. It was about two when I blinked for what seemed like the first time in hours and realized I had been sitting on the couch not doing anything.

I took a deep breath and headed to the bathroom, finally looking at myself for the first time. Thank goodness no one except Maeve saw me today. I looked like hell. I hopped in the shower and let the hot water run on me for as long as I could. Taking extra time to wash my hair and shave my legs. I seemed to have run out of tears so I dragged myself out of the shower and put on clothes for the day. I needed to take a walk, get something to eat and get my head on straight.

I went downstairs, trying not to make eye contact, but I told Maeve I was going for a walk and wouldn't be home for dinner. I heard her say something about giving it time, but it didn't process in my brain. I headed into the woods to the prayer building. I lay on one of the benches and looked up through the glass ceiling, watching the leaves blow in the breeze. I started giving myself a pep talk. I told myself that three and a half months wasn't a lot of time and I needed to enjoy my time here while I had the chance. I told myself that it could include Sean as a friend, but I would allow myself a few days to get through the awkward part of the breakup. He would, of course, be in my life, I lived with his parents for crying out loud, but we could be adults about this. *Couldn't we?*

A few hours later, I had talked myself into what had to happen and made a plan for the rest of my time here. It made me feel grounded and stable and I felt like me again. I didn't know what was going to happen when I saw him next, but I would cross that bridge when I came to it.

23

A week went by before I had to find out how awkward our next meeting would be. Sean had left it up to me if I wanted to contact him. I noticed Maeve was missing him and I felt guilty for him not coming over so I offered to invite him over for dinner one night. Maeve beamed but gently asked if I would be okay with that. I told her I thought so and I didn't want to stand in the way of her seeing him so, if it got bad, I would retreat to the upstairs or go for a walk.

I sent Sean a text. I told him I wanted to try to be friends and that his mom was missing him. I asked him to come to dinner tomorrow night. He sent a smiling emoji and said that he would be happy to come to dinner. He asked if he could bring anything. I told him just to bring himself. He asked me if it would be all right if we met tonight, just the two of us. He didn't want our first meeting since the breakup to be in front of his parents and didn't want it to be weird. I agreed and told him I would meet him at the bridge over the river at seven tonight.

I filled Maeve in on the plan for tomorrow night and she set about making a grocery list for tomorrow night's dinner and started to fuss. I left her to it and went to help Tom with closing the store. We finished up downstairs and I couldn't help but be nervous about tonight. I didn't eat much and it was noticed but no one said anything. I told them I was going for a walk and went up to get my jacket.

    I got to the bridge at a quarter-to-seven. I looked out at the sunset, kicking myself for picking a place that was romantic, but I figured it would be better to be out in the open and not at the pub or the prayer house. Sean pulled up and parked. I saw him in my periphery taking a deep breath and running his hands through his hair. He opened the door and stepped out. I turned my head and waved hesitantly. He waved back and walked up. He started to lean in to kiss my cheek but thought better of it and stopped short. He put his hand out in front of him and said, "Good evening," with a smirk on his face. I placed my hand in his and shook it, but it felt so wrong. Not wanting to give him the wrong impression, I started to try to explain how maybe a friendly hug would be less awkward as long as he didn't read too much into it. His smirk became a smile and he pulled my hand gently. He offered me a quick hug that made me feel a little better and I pointed to the bridge, asking if he would like to sit.

    We sat down next to each other, though I left some space between us this time. I asked how his week was and he told me it was a rough one but he managed to wrap his head around it. I told him it was the same for me. We talked about work and fell into easy conversation. Being friends with Sean might not be so hard, though I did find myself missing his touch. Our conversation grew quiet, and I figured it was time to call it a night before our conversation got heavy. I thanked him for understanding and told him I had to head back. He said he understood and thanked me for still wanting to be his friend. I hugged him goodnight and walked back to The Turning Page alone, even though he had offered me the ride.

I locked up the store and headed upstairs, feeling better about tomorrow. I said goodnight to Tom who was sitting at the kitchen table as I walked up the stairs. He said goodnight back and mentioned Maeve left me a small plate of food and a bit of the dessert she had made. I stopped on the stairs as my stomach rumbled and walked over for the plates. I asked if Maeve had gone to bed. Tom said she had so I slipped the dessert plate in front of him and told him he could have it as I walked upstairs with the other plate. I saw him lean back just a bit to see if Maeve could see him and then dug into the chocolate tart. I smiled at him and he winked at me. I went upstairs and got ready for bed between bites of food. A small sigh of relief escaped my lips as I slipped into bed.

24

The next morning, I woke very rested and ready for the day. I was in the kitchen making eggs and country potatoes before Maeve and Tom got out of bed. They were dressed for the day and came out in search of tea and breakfast. Tom sat down with a huge smile on his face and a fork in his hand. Maeve quietly sat down when I wouldn't let her help and picked up the paper that I brought in from the front porch. While serving up breakfast, I thanked the two of them for being so patient with me. I knew it wasn't easy not seeing Sean this week. Tom tucked into his food and didn't say much. Maeve gave him a disapproving look and reached for my hand and patted it. She told me things would work themselves out and sipped her tea. I told them that I could handle the store if they wanted to take today off. Tom mentioned needing to get some items for their trip to the Faroe Islands in August. He said they could go to Galway and hit the shops. Maeve smiled and said she needed to get a baby gift for Molly too. Molly was due in a few months and Maeve wanted to have something for her before the shower. I asked Maeve if she happened to see any soft yarn if she would please pick some up for me and

I would work on a baby blanket for the baby while I was here. She asked if I crocheted or knitted. I told her I could do both but not very well. I was mostly proficient at rectangles so scarfs and baby blankets are all I could do. She told me she had crochet hooks I could use and I beamed with excitement. I hadn't made a baby blanket in a while and it would be fun. It would also give me something to work on since I wouldn't be out with Sean at night.

They made their plans as we finished eating and I ran upstairs to get some money for Maeve then I headed down to the shop to open. The sun was out and the sky was a gorgeous blue. There were only a few puffy white clouds in the sky. I opened the front door and propped it open with a flowerpot, letting a light breeze float in. There were a few tourists walking up and down the sidewalks waiting for shops to open with takeaway cups of coffee in hand. Maeve and Tom came down, ready for their shopping trip to Galway. Maeve brought me a brown bag with snacks and a sandwich for lunch. She said they should be back before dinner. It was supposed to be a beautiful day, so I wished them safe travels from the register as a man and a woman entered the shop with their three kids. Maeve looked back with a, "we should stay," look on her face, but I waved them goodbye, and Tom steered her toward their car.

The man and woman were definitely tourists. They had American accents. I wandered over to see if they needed help finding anything and the woman looked relieved to hear someone with an American accent too. I pointed to the children's book section and offered that we had small plush toys to go with some of the books. Her three children, whom I would guess were all under the age of eight, were full of energy. It reminded me of Sam when she was little but there was only one of her, so I walked them over to the section and showed them what we had. The woman explained to me that the kids or maybe it was the parents hadn't quite gotten used to the time change yet, so they were in need of a walk to work out some of that energy. I mentioned the walk to the castle and her two little boys stopped in their tracks.

"A real live castle?" they asked excitedly. They were all ears so I explained the road and the guard tower and the grounds of the castle. I mentioned the equestrian center and that got the oldest child, the daughter's attention. Then I mentioned the hawks and the castle restaurants. The whole family beamed. Each child picked out a book and a plush toy to go with it. The woman picked up some souvenirs and the man picked up a book on Ashford Castle, though he said something about having to wait to read it until the littles were all in bed. I rang them up and then walked them out the door. I pointed them in the direction of the road, thanked them for coming in and hoped that they had a great vacation.

The rest of the morning was steady, busy. A couple of orders came in and there were enough browsing customers to keep me occupied. The Armstrongs came in shortly after I opened the box with an order for them in it. They left quickly, wanting to be away from the crowds. There were a few other orders so I sorted them and made phone calls between customers. One order was for Phyllis so I called Arthur to let him know. He had some bad news, Phyllis was not doing well and moving her from the bed to the wheelchair was uncomfortable for her. The nurses didn't recommend her coming out for the next couple of weeks until they could make better arrangements. I asked if there was anything I could do, offering to bring her the order if she could have visitors. Arthur asked the nurse and she said it would be all right this afternoon if I didn't stay too long. They wanted her to rest and get some strength back.

    The afternoon was quiet so I gathered up a few book recommendations for Phyllis along with her order and had them ready for my visit. I had called Maeve and told her what was happening. She told me that they would be back by three and they would watch the store so I could go see her. When they returned, Tom came in with two handfuls of bags from their shopping trip. Maeve had a small gift that was wrapped and some flowers for Phyllis. Once Tom came down to watch the shop, I bagged up everything and headed out the door. Word got around quickly in a small town, and as I passed a few shops, the owners asked if I was going to see Phyllis and if I would take her a gift from them. By the time I made it to Phyllis's home, I was loaded down with food, treats, gifts, cards, and flowers. Arthur answered the door with his eyes wide. I explained the last few minutes of my walk to him and he helped me put things down. We organized the pile of well wishes and decided that it would be overwhelming for her to get it all at once. Arthur offered to give her something each day to help pass the time. Phyllis was well-loved by the town as evidenced by the bounty. I had her order and the flowers and gift from Maeve in hand when I went into her room. She looked very tired but perked up a bit with the visit. I handed her the gift from Maeve and set the flowers in a vase that Arthur had brought in. As she opened the gift, I set her order on the table next to the bed and held onto the suggestion books I brought. Maeve had picked out a beautiful little hummingbird suncatcher made of green and purple glass. Phyllis was delighted. She asked if I could hang it in the window next to the bed. I pulled some of the stuffing out of the box and found the suction cup inside. Hanging it in the window, it caught the afternoon sun and cast green and purple sparkles on the far wall.

We talked for a few minutes and she tried to hide the pain she was in. I showed her a few suggestions and she had me put a couple on hold for next time. I told her one of us at the book shop would be glad to make the trip to see her once a week and bring her what she would like. Arthur thanked me and said it would help keep her spirits up until they could get back out on the road again. Arthur told Phyllis of all the other gifts and she was happy to have such good friends nearby. She said she was too tired to see everything now but that maybe after her nap he could bring her a card or two.

I said my goodbyes and told Phyllis that one of us would be by next week to visit with the next book she had on hold. Arthur gave me money for that book as I left. He told me to bring back the change with the book next week and not to worry about bringing it back today. My trip back to The Turning Page was as long as my trip there. Everyone wanted to know how she was doing. I told them she was in good spirits but tired easily and that they should take turns visiting so she didn't get worn out. They all agreed and I'm sure the phone calls started. I felt for the nurses, they would have to come up with a visitation schedule.

I was back inside The Turning Page for only a second before Maeve was asking for an update. I relayed what I saw and heard and what was said. Maeve seemed to calm a little.

"Phyllis is very dear to the town," Maeve said, "I don't know what we will do when she leaves us to be with Harold again." I gave Maeve a hug and told her that I hoped we had many years before that happened.

Tom and I closed up the store at six in the evening and Maeve was busy bustling in the kitchen. I offered to help and was tasked with the vegetables. Maeve was doing a fish fry with chips and a salad with tons of veggies. She had canned Guinness and Jameson and ginger ale on the sideboard. It smelled amazing in the kitchen when Sean arrived. You could tell he missed his mom's cooking. He brought her flowers and asked about Phyllis. Maeve had Tom set the table while I relayed my visit with Phyllis.

Sean said he would send flowers in a couple of days, giving time for her current flowers to need refreshing. Phyllis was his primary school teacher so he held a special place in his heart for her.

Dinner was delicious, with only a few awkward moments here and there, where Sean caught me staring at him or I caught him staring at me. I missed him but it was for the best. Or at least that was what I told myself. Maeve asked, with an eye on Sean, about my next day off and what I had planned. It was in a few days and I planned on spending it in the library at Ashford, hopefully, finishing Last September. Sean offered that I was welcome to visit the birds. Fern was back in rotation, her babies were learning to fly and Archimedes was bound to need some cuddles. I smiled and said I would see what the day held. Maeve seemed satisfied after that so she brought out dessert. She baked chocolate chip cookies and had a container of vanilla ice cream. Tom volunteered to scoop the ice cream, mostly so he could lick the scoop when he was finished. Maeve took the bowls of ice cream and added two cookies then passed them out. We sat down and I took one cookie, placed the scoop of ice cream on it and added the second cookie to make a sandwich. Pleased with myself for thinking of it, I looked up and noticed that every one of us was holding an ice cream sandwich. We looked from one to another and I started laughing. After dessert, I offered to clean up the kitchen while the rest caught up with each other. I managed to stay out of the way and out of the conversation which I was pleased about. I finished up and told everyone I had some phone calls to make and said goodnight. Sean started to get up but I moved to the stairs quickly and was, thankfully, upstairs before he could say anything.

In my room, I threw on some pajamas and took my hair out and brushed it. I had it in braids today so it was a curly, fluffy mess. I scooped it up into a bun.

I found a bag with yarn, some change from the money I gave to Maeve and her crochet hooks on the bed. The yarn was beautiful and so soft. Maeve chose yarn that was a mix of lavenders and greens. I dialed Sam on video chat as I settled onto the bed, laying out the yarn and starting my first chain. I seemed to catch her mid-sentence. She didn't even say hi. It was like I joined the conversation by walking up next to her. It made me smile. She was talking with Jake and Mom about wedding details. Jake was just nodding and Mom was shooting a word in here and there. Sam has had her entire wedding planned since the first wedding dress-up kit she ever received for Christmas when she was five. I could only imagine poor Jake when she got him into a tux shop. Sam finally finished the story of her vision for the wedding and acknowledged that I had joined the conversation. I asked how things were going and if they had set a date yet? Sam told me they had narrowed it down to three dates, one next year and two the following year, so there was plenty of time to take Jake to all the bridal boutiques and seminars she could find. I saw Jake roll his eyes and I stifled a laugh. I asked how Mom was and she took the phone from Sam. Mom stepped into the other room and took a deep breath. Sometimes Sam was too much for her. I asked if she was okay. Mom laughed and sighed at the same time and said that Samantha would have this thing planned before I got home. I laughed. *That might not be a bad thing.*

Mom noticed the yarn and asked what I was making. I told her it was, hopefully, going to be a baby blanket for a new friend here. She asked about the stitch pattern and wanted to see the colors better. I obliged. Once Mom was satisfied in my pattern choice and my first three rows were completed, she let me get off the phone. I set my project down and said my good nights and wished them all good afternoons. Lying in bed, my heart had started aching. *He was right downstairs and all I had to do was go to him. But I couldn't do that to him, couldn't do that to me, could I?* I turned over and willed myself to go to sleep.

25

A few days later, I took my day off. I slept in a bit just because I could and then started my day. Showered, dressed, and backpack ready with a rain jacket and umbrella, I headed down to the kitchen. The teapot was on the counter and I added some to my travel mug. I snagged a piece of bacon and a scone for breakfast. A brown bag was on the counter. I didn't even bother to look inside. I put an apple in the pocket of my backpack and filled my water bottle.

Romping through the forest for a few hours did me good. The fresh air and creatures scurrying helped me clear my head. Though I thought about Sean almost nonstop, I mostly convinced myself we could just be friends despite how badly I missed him, especially at night. During the day I was fine with the idea of friends, but deep down, I ached for him to hold me again. His eyes told me that he still wanted me but was being patient for me. Seeing him the other night was good and bad. I just wished I could figure out a way for it to work but we just didn't live in the same country.

I spent the whole day in the forest enjoying nature and battling my demons. By the end of the day, with the setting sun turning the sky brilliant oranges and pinks, I had still not gotten any closer to a solution that meant Sean and I could be together.

26

A few weeks later, with summer in full swing, the book shop was busy every day. I had made a few visits to see Phyllis in between the rest of the town visiting. Maeve, Tom, and Sean all visited as well. Phyllis had good days and bad. The weather warmed up, even though I was still wearing cardigans with all my t-shirts. The rain came less during the days but there were always water drops on the flowers in the mornings.

Sean and I spent a lot of time together, becoming closer friends, even though it was clear he wanted more. It was different but it felt right to have him in my life. Maeve was happier too now that we had found a balance.

Today was my day off so Sean added me to the list of riders for this afternoon and I made plans to go see Archimedes before the ride. So, with most of my afternoon planned, I got up early for some "me" time. I dressed, packed my backpack with all my "just in cases", and went down for breakfast. Tom and Maeve were just getting up, so we moved methodically around each other. I packed my own snacks for the day while Maeve made breakfast and Tom prepared the tea. We all sat at once, each serving ourselves and passing the eggs, bacon, and toast around. We talked about the shop and about a couple of special orders that came in late yesterday. I hadn't made the phone calls yet, so Tom said he would take care of it.

We finished breakfast and I helped clean up, then headed out for the day. The morning would be for exploring. One of the entries in the past employee journal in my room mentioned Pigeon Hole Cave and I wanted to see it. I walked down to the abbey and through the gray stones. I went across the bright green grass and crossed the stone bridge at the fishing house. I saw some fish in the water, they glistened in the sunlight. I turned right and easily found the trail, following the red arrows through the forest that clearly marked the trail. The forest was beautiful green trees, ferns, and moss everywhere. The green seemed to get more vibrant as the seasons progressed.

I crossed the road and came to a tunnel and followed the path. It was well-marked and only took about a half-an-hour to get to the cave.

I wasn't the first one there though; a group of five backpackers were already there. There were three girls and two boys all dressed in brightly colored hiking gear, their backpacks sitting near their feet. It made me feel a little unprepared for the hike down the stone steps when I saw they all had headlamp lights attached to their heads or hats. Hellos were exchanged as I walked up and set my backpack down. I reached in my pack for my handheld flashlight and made sure everything I might need was easily reachable.

One of the female backpackers got everyone's attention and started to read from her phone. She read the history of the area and the legend of Pigeon Hole Cave. She smiled at me as I sat on the ground to listen to the story. She was enthusiastic about the history of the area and all but acted out the characters of the legend. The story was about a beautiful woman who was betrothed to a prince. That prince was murdered before they could wed and she was heartbroken. It wasn't long before the woman disappeared. It was said she was taken by the fairies and turned into a white trout that could be found in the river inside the cave. The story continued with a soldier coming to see if the uncatchable white trout rumors were true. He did catch the trout and tried to eat it, stabbing it with a knife. The fish screamed and transformed back into the woman. She told him her story and said she was waiting for her true love. She demanded to be returned to the river, and to this day, it was said that you could sometimes find a white trout with a scar swimming in the cave. The storyteller had a flair for the dramatic and it was very entertaining to watch. When she was done, her group and I applauded for her performance. She took a bow and the group stood up and put on their backpacks. I stepped forward and offered to take a group picture of them outside and inside the cave, if they let me tag along with their group for a little bit. They agreed and the storyteller handed me her phone and introduced herself as Madeline

Dearborn. I snapped a few photos of the group. Some smiling, others silly. Then they each took turns introducing themselves. I would probably never remember all of their names, but Madeline accepted her phone back and called out for one more picture with me in it. I did my best to hide in the back.

The six of us walked carefully down the stone stairs, not really needing the flashlights yet. The walls of the stairway were speckled with moss and ferns, the steps were covered in last year's fallen leaves, so they were slippery. There was a handrail to help get down, which was thoughtful of whoever had it installed. The soft, green, spongy moss continued inside to the walls at the opening of the cave where the light could reach. The cave was only dark in some spaces as there was a hole in the top of the cave that let the sunlight shine down on the river. I snapped a few photos of my own, then swapped phones with Madeline so I could get some non-selfie photos of myself in the cave. I took several photos of their group then we switched phones back again. They had a couple of adventurous people in their group who wanted to see where the cave went. I was content with the stream and the light dancing on it and waved them on. I took a few more photos and listened to their laughs echoing in the cave along with some splashing. I could hear that other people had arrived at the cave up above, and having had my fill of social interactions with strangers, I called out to Madeline and told them I was leaving. They all said goodbye at once then Madeline called out that they would be in town tonight and planned on eating dinner and getting drinks at the Crow's Nest, if I wanted to join them. I thanked her, told her I would see what I could do, and waved goodbye.

A family, two men and three kids, came down the stairs as I turned to leave. We said hellos as we passed each other and I heard one of the daughters gasp as she slipped on the wet stairs. One of the dads caught her before she hurt herself. I heard one of them remind everyone to be careful on the steps.

I survived my climb up the stone steps and back to the expansive green that was the forest. It was time to head to the castle for my date with Archimedes. It took me a little over an hour-and-a-half to get to the falconry. I stopped along the route to take in the forest, passing people on the trail occasionally. I avoided accidental photobombing when possible. I made it back to the abbey and turned right. I saw Molly was out for a walk and I caught up to her easily. She had just under two months left and was trying to stay active. I asked how she had been feeling and she told me she was tired but feeling good. Though it was getting harder every day to pick up the things she had dropped. She said that this little girl inside her was very active. She took my hand and rested it on her stomach for a few minutes.

I didn't feel anything moving and she frowned. "She never moves when I want her to. It must be her personality, just like her da, already coming through." I laughed. I told her I had been working on a gift for her and that I was almost done. She lit up and told me that her mom and

Maeve were working on the baby shower, it was next week, and she would make sure I was on the guest list. Then she asked how long I would be in Ireland. I said I had to go home early September. She frowned but then smiled and said that I would still be here when she had the baby.

A few minutes later, Molly said she'd reached the halfway point in her walk. She hugged me and turned around, heading back home and I continued on to the castle. I skirted the front of the castle and wound around to the falconry. I stepped into the main lobby and said hi to George. He came around the counter and gave me a hug. I asked if it was all right if I went to get Archimedes to hold for a bit, promising I would bring him into the lobby and tell them both about my morning. He handed me a glove as I set down my pack behind the counter, then I walked down to Archimedes' enclosure. I put a small piece of chicken in the palm of my glove and stepped inside the enclosure. I whistled a pathetic sound and Archimedes perked up and flew to my glove. It was a really good thing he was food motivated and I just needed to get his attention. He took his snack then walked up my arm towards my elbow. I stroked his chest and head and told him to be good and not fly away while we walked back to the lobby as I didn't have a leather tie for his leg.

I closed his enclosure and walked back to the lobby. George was checking in a couple for their hawk walk when I came back, so I stepped behind the counter and tucked in the corner. As George was talking to the customers, he pointed at Archimedes and whistled. I lifted my arm slightly. Archimedes launched from my arm and swooped around the room, landing on the perch on the counter. George introduced the couple to him and told them that the birds they would be walking with today didn't like to be petted like him so it was best to keep their fingers away from their beaks. The woman asked if she could pet Archimedes and George showed her how. After a few minutes, George showed Archimedes a piece of chicken and tossed it to me. Archimedes hopped across the counter and flapped his wings, sending a bit of paperwork fluttering to the ground before he got airborne for a minute and landed back on my glove. George said something I think was a cuss word in Gaelic and picked up the mess. I laughed and cuddled in the corner with my date while George finished the paperwork. Sean walked into the lobby a few minutes later to take the couple on their walk and saw me. He smiled, ushering the couple out the door and asked if I wanted to join them. I didn't feel right taking over the walk that they paid for and told him I would pass but I would see him that afternoon for our ride. He said he had arranged for me to ride Millie.

I sat in the lobby with Archimedes and talked with George for over an hour, telling him about my day and he told me about his week. George and I were eating lunch when the couple came back from their hawk walk with glowing smiles. They scheduled another walk in a couple of days, before they had to head home and thanked George and Sean for the amazing time. Sean grabbed his lunch from the fridge in the breakroom and joined us in the lobby. I told Sean about the cave that morning and he told George and I about the walk with the couple and how they were having such a good time that he had kept them out for a little longer than usual in the hopes that they would book another.

After we all finished our lunches, I said goodbye to George and then Sean and I took Archimedes back to his enclosure. Then Sean offered to take me to the stables with the golf cart. I accepted and we walked over to where it was parked. When we arrived at the equestrian center, Millie and Cara were saddled and ready for us. There was a group getting ready and Sean helped me with my gear. I asked if he was coming with us and he told me that the group was going with John but that I was going with him. I gave him a skeptical look and he put his hands up and said he just wanted to try a new trail with the horses to see how they did. *This would be the first time on a horse in a long time so I would rather not have had an audience.* I agreed to go with him.

Millie was so gentle compared to Cara, who needed a run. While I got myself situated on Millie, Sean got Cara ready for the ride. He checked her tack and she was antsy to get going, so we headed out to an open area just outside the equestrian center fences. I let Millie have her reins and she milled about the grass, munching quietly. All my anxiety seems to disappear, knowing Millie would take care of me. I told Sean that Cara needed to run and he agreed so he nudged her into a canter and then to a full gallop. She flew around the open area and both she and

Sean seemed to enjoy the freedom. I smiled as I watched them circle the area, feeling their energy as they rushed by. Millie was unfazed and munched on the grass. Not wanting to interrupt Millie's grazing but really wanting to join in, I gently picked up the reins and she seemed to understand. We followed the path in the clearing at a cantor, Sean passed me again as Millie and I got a feel for each other's responses. Sean got close to passing again so I tapped Millie's flanks with my heels. She responded and we galloped around the area enjoying the lightness of the afternoon. Cara had a longer stride so they caught up quickly. We both reined in the horses to a trot, and I asked where the trail was that he wanted to try, now that Cara had settled a bit.

He pointed to an opening in the tree line and we nudged the horses in that direction. We quickly found a path through the vast forest but it was almost untouched by man. There were no visible trails that had been traversed before us. It was quiet as the horses picked their way between the trees. Creatures scampered as we created our own trail, letting Millie follow Cara at her own pace. It wasn't long before I was completely lost. Sean was still in front of me, leading the way but I couldn't tell you what direction the castle was in or where the river was. I heard a raven caw and saw it land on a nearby tree. It hopped a few times and ruffled its feathers before it settled in, content to watch us from a distance.

Sean stopped at a small meadow hidden in the forest, I pulled Millie to a stop next to him. His face was glowing with excitement, he told me he was thinking of bringing horses and hawks here for a combined tour. He hopped down off his saddle and helped me down from mine. We walked the meadow, letting the horses graze on the grass while we explored the area. He pointed out places in the trees the hawks could perch and described how they would fly down to us over the meadow, dipping and gliding along the way. It sounded so wonderful. I could picture it all.

Sean slipped his hand in mine and squeezed as I squeezed back once and started to pull away.

He held a little tighter and asked me, "If I lived in California or you lived here, would we still be together?" Millie nudged me in the arm. Looking at her, I bought myself a moment to collect my thoughts. *Oh! Yes! But do I say that? Honesty and truth are always best.* I gave a soft yes and looked down. He reached for my other hand and took Millie's reins, putting them and Cara's in the hand that was holding mine. He reached for my chin and lifted it slightly. I looked up into his blue gray eyes, the color of a storm on the sea, he saw the tears pooling in mine. I didn't know what to say.

He smiled slightly, kissed me lightly on the nose, and told me, "It's going to work out, love. I just need to know the hurdles so I can get us over them." I started to ask one of the hundred questions in my head and he placed his finger over my lips. "I'm not going to give up on you as long as there is hope," he said with a "take your breath away" smile and squeezed my hand. He handed me back Millie's reins and helped me back on her saddle. As he stepped into Cara's stirrup and swung his leg over, he said, "Besides, stubbornness is a virtue of the Irish."

"I don't think it's ever been called a virtue before," I said as I smiled and rolled my eyes.

We headed back to the stables. I offered to wipe down and brush Millie but the stable hand, Aidan, would have none of it. Sean offered to take me back to The Turning Page and I accepted. He called Maeve on the way to his lorry and told her we were on our way. She had dinner started when we arrived. Tom was finishing up the closing procedures. Sean stayed downstairs to help Tom and I went upstairs to see if Maeve needed help. Maeve shooed me upstairs to shower because I smelled like horses. She yelled down to Sean to use the shower in their room if he planned to eat tonight. I smiled at the thought of him being sent home for not coming to the table presentable, knowing full well it would never happen.

I found a change of clothes and headed to the bathroom. My thoughts went back to the moment in the meadow as the warm water ran in rivers down my body. *What am I doing? This is never going to work. Less than six weeks left! What am I thinking?*

"I'm thinking I want him to tear off all my clothes and never leave Ireland again!" I say out loud and jolt out of my thoughts. I shook my head. *I'm hopeless!*

I went through the motions of shampoo, conditioner, and soap. *Is that really what I wanted? Could I give up my life at home? My family? Leave everything behind? For a guy? For THE guy? Is he my person? What am I going to do? This wouldn't be so hard if I didn't love him so much! But I do. There, in the shower, contemplating my life, I could see how things would be so good for us. We could make it work if we, I don't know, lived on the same continent!*

Frustrated, I finished rinsing off and turned off the water. I would love to see my daydream become reality, but I just didn't know how that could work with us living on opposite sides of the globe.

I brushed the whole thing aside in my head and finished getting dressed. I combed out my hair and threw it up into a librarian bun. I grabbed my blush brush and attacked my cheeks and eyelids with just what was on the brush then added a few swipes of mascara then headed down for dinner. The smells from the kitchen wafted up the stairs. Garlic and lemon fish with rice and broccoli. There was a salad and two bottles of crisp Sauvignon Blanc on the table.

We talked about our days over dinner. They had a great day at the store. It was busy for most of the day except around lunch when most of the visitors were in the pubs and restaurants. Maeve said that she spent a half hour with Phyllis today. She was not doing as well as the nurses would like and they didn't expect her to get better. Maeve told us that the nurses had switched to maintenance and comfort instead of working to get her moving again. She said she overheard the nurse making notes into a recording device while she was in visiting Phyllis.

I mentioned making our visits shorter but more often than once a week and we all agreed. I said I would go visit the day after tomorrow. Sean said he would bring over some flowers tomorrow for me to take for my visit.

We all had a bit of heaviness weighing on our minds because of Phyllis. Maeve cleaned the kitchen around me as I did the dishes. Tom and Sean sat quietly at the table. Maeve asked if anyone was interested in going out for a drink and maybe some music tonight to drive away the melancholy. I remembered the invitation from Madeline and mentioned it. Everyone seemed to get their second wind.

Maeve said, "Well, that settles it. I'm going to change my shirt and get my coat. Let's go have some craic!"

I went upstairs to do the same and then we walked to the Crow's Nest. It was brighter inside than I expected. The wood bar was right in front of you when you walked in. It was a medium brown and the walls were a light sage green. There were several windows that would let some natural light in during the day and plenty of lighting for the evenings. They had scattered tall tables in front of the bar, a small nook to the left of the bar with low tables and chairs, and a larger area to the right of the bar with more tables and chairs. It was busy but we managed to find Madeline and her friends. They bought us a round of drinks and regaled us with stories from their day. There was music all around us. The lift in our spirits did us good.

We relaxed into the music and the evening. Madeline slid up next to me and asked me about Sean. She asked how long we'd been together. I was taken aback. I stammered out something about being just friends and me leaving in less than six weeks.

Madeline looked at me with knowing eyes and said, "uh huh, does he know that?" with a small gesture towards Sean. I followed her move and caught his eye across the space. He gave a big grin, tipped his hat, and winked at me. I flushed and looked away. Madeline laughed and whispered, "Oh! You've both got it bad! Cheer up!" she said as she tapped her glass with mine, "If it's right it will work out. If it's not, then take the time you get. He's so freaking hot!"

I changed the subject and asked which one was hers, pointing to her group of friends. She smiled and pointed to the tallest. "That's Will, isn't he gorgeous? We're getting married, he doesn't know it yet though," she said in my ear. We both let out a giggle. Will and Madeline made eye contact and she nudged me with her elbow as she walked away from me towards him. I nuzzled back against the wall and took in the atmosphere, the alcohol doing its job, my head began to swim. I sat my glass down and decided to end my evening. I wandered slowly around the group saying goodnight to everyone. Maeve and Tom said they would join me and Sean followed us out.

He said he would be back after work tomorrow with flowers for Phyllis and said goodnight to us. We walked back to The Turning Page. Maeve hugged me and said she was off to bed and Tom followed. I went upstairs and texted my dad, my mom and sister, telling them I would call tomorrow after work. I changed my pants, took off my bra, and crawled into bed.

27

I left the shop two days later around one p.m., with flowers, a small box of candy, and the latest book in the series Phyllis was reading. Knocking on the door, I said a small prayer that I wasn't interrupting anything and that Phyllis was awake.

She greeted me with a soft smile as I entered her bedroom. I smiled back but it wasn't convincing because she motioned for me to come sit next to her on the bed.

"Don't you be shedding any tears for me. I've lived a wonderful life, my dear. Everyone's time comes." A small cough escaped her lips as she patted my hand. "I see you brought some goodies for me. The blooms are lovely."

I settled my items on the bed and moved the flowers to the bedside table. They filled the air with sweet floral smells. I showed her the candy and she took them and put them under her pillow.

"These will give me sweet dreams, to be sure." I smiled and showed her the new book and she was happy because they had just finished the last one, but she wasn't up for a story just now. We set the book next to the flowers and she took my hands in hers. Her fingers looked so frail.

She squeezed my hands and in a soft voice said, "Life goes by so quickly. You have to take all the opportunities that come your way, no matter how scary or impossible they seem. Sean loves you and I can see you love him too! You hold onto that and don't let go! Things have a way of working out when it's right."

I squeezed her hands gently and whispered, "I hope you're right."

I left a short while later when Phyllis yawned for the fifth time. I mentioned to her nurse that the box of candy under her pillow might melt before she gets to them.

The nurse said," I will go find it but I'll make sure she knows where it's at. No point in holding back the good stuff at the end." It caught me off-guard.

I asked tentatively, "Is it the end?"

"Aye, lass, but we'll keep her comfortable until then. We've transferred her to hospice care instead of recuperation," the nurse said as she walked me to the door. "Don't you worry about Miss Phyllis. She's had a grand life and she has lots of family and friends to keep her days full. Arthur comes tomorrow to visit her."

I returned to The Turning Page mechanically. I walked in the door and Maeve and Katherine Armstrong were waiting with bated breath to hear how Phyllis was doing. Katherine was in the store with Donnie but she saw me walk past the window and gathered with Maeve near the front door to hear the news firsthand. Maeve saw my face and called out to Tom to close up the shop, meet us at Pat Cohan's, and bring Donnie. Maeve and Katherine guided me to the pub, ordered three Guinnesses, and sat me down in a booth. Maeve reached for my hand and asked what news I had. Katherine slid in the booth next to me. Maeve mentioned to Katherine the visit with Phyllis a couple of days ago and there was no change in her status. I told both ladies what the nurse had told me, that Phyllis was accepting of the inevitable, and added that we should be prepared to lose Phyllis in the near future. Having not been old enough when my grandparents died, I wasn't sure how to cope with a loss of someone so dear. The beers arrived at the table and Tom and Donnie showed up a few minutes later. I retold what the nurse told me and then sat back and let the rest of the table talk. Lost in my thoughts about Phyllis and what she said, I drank my beer down and listened to the two couples at the table. Maeve set another Guinness in front of me and called to Jerry for another round for the table.

    The stories went from concerned conversations to stories of Phyllis's life and how she played major roles in every person's life at the table. Katherine and Maeve made a plan to visit this week. I let them know that Arthur would be visiting tomorrow. More beer came to the table as the night progressed. I managed a quick text to Sean, letting him know what was happening. He asked if I needed him to rescue me and I told him I wasn't sure how long they planned to be there, but I was at least four Guinnesses in with no food. About fifteen minutes later, Sean walked through the door and ordered a beer on the way to the table. He pulled a chair from another table and sat at the end of the booth. Jerry brought Sean his beer and a charcuterie board for the table. We snacked and talked some more after the ladies filled Sean in. Using the excuse of needing the water closet (the bathroom), I managed to switch seats and get the outside seat at the booth. Sean then ordered a few more appetizers for the table and paid the bill off before asking me if I would like to go for a walk. I accepted, leaving the rest of the table to their food, another round, and their stories.

Sean asked how I was doing as we walked toward the bookstore, and having had too many drinks, I felt silly and replied with a slurring of the word, "fine". He had a grin on his face and nodded without arguing with me when we reached the front door. We wound our way through the store and stopped on the second floor. Sean made some tea and there were scones leftover from breakfast under the cloche dish on the table. I sat at the table, and he brought over two cups of tea and some butter, cream, and jam. I leaned against the table and swirled my spoon in my cup. It dawned on me that the news about Phyllis might hit Sean pretty hard too, so I asked how he was doing.

He smiled and said, "she's not gone yet, so we have the days the Lord will give us."

I sipped my tea, and because I was drunk and couldn't stop my mouth, I asked why he was so great. He smiled and patiently said, "It's just who I am, love." I had an overwhelming urge to kiss him, but I chased a bite of scone with some tea and realized I was not sober and decisions about kissing are best left to sober minds. I looked at him and asked if it was too early for bed. He asked if I needed to shower with a twinkle in his eye. As I thought about it, he told me he was only teasing. I asked if he would spend the night or go home. He asked what I would like him to do. I was just drunk enough to ask him to stay but I hesitated, saying nothing. He stood up, kissed me on the forehead, and escorted me to the staircase. He told me that it was not quite bedtime, but we could watch something on the telly upstairs before I went to bed. Then he said he would stay until I went to bed, but he would go home for the night.

He sent me to put on my pajamas while he found something on TV. Without thinking too much, I changed and went out to the couch. Sean was there, looking perfect with an arm open for me to slide into. I was just foggy enough not to overthink it and settled into the crook of his arm. I couldn't tell you what was on TV but being curled up in his arms was so wonderful that I fell asleep in no time. Sean woke me up a short time later and walked me to bed. He kissed my forehead, I leaned into a tight hug, and because I was still drunk, I couldn't stop my mouth when I told him that Phyllis said he loved me and that she could tell I loved him. He asked me if I thought that was true. I told him I did think it was true and asked if he thought the same. He told me it was true. I told him that Phyllis said things have a way of working out when it's right and that I should hold on to us. He held me tighter and said that he'd been saying that for a while now. I kissed his cheek, then crawled into bed and fell asleep as Sean closed the door.

28

The next morning the alarm went off too soon. The headache that registered a minute later was enough to tell me I needed water. I padded to the bathroom and got some water and some aspirin as I searched my memory for holes from last night. Something Sean had said resonated with me. "She's not gone yet so we have the days the Lord will give us." *We all only have the days the Lord will give us regardless of our age. Not just Phyllis but everyone… What have I been doing? Wasting my time here and with Sean because I'm afraid of getting hurt.* As I confronted the me in the mirror, I stared her down. When I saw Phyllis next, she was going to know I was done being scared!

I jumped into the shower and felt the tension and the headache dissipate with the help of the aspirin and the hot water. I got dressed and headed down to the kitchen. There was a mound of peaches on the counter in the fruit basket, so I decided on peach crumble pie for dessert and peach pancakes with a bourbon maple syrup for breakfast. I made one big batch of cut up peaches with sugar and cinnamon then separated them into two bowls. I made a pie crust and put it in the fridge to rest while I mixed the crumble topping and then made the pancake batter. I mixed up some maple syrup with a splash or two of bourbon, careful to not smell it too deeply. Then I heated up the griddle and started the pancake circles. I topped each pancake with three slices of peaches and flipped them when they were ready. I continued to do that until all the batter was gone and set them on the table with the butter and the syrup. Tom's nose woke his stomach up and he was poking around the kitchen for tea fixings and plates when Maeve made her way to the table. She looked a little worse for wear and opted for the non-bourbon maple syrup. Tom and his iron stomach had no problem with anything he ate. We sat and ate quietly. Once the food and tea settled, we talked about last night. I repeated what Sean had said and both Tom and Maeve agreed. I got up and Tom jumped out of his seat to help. It looked like Maeve might have kicked him a bit but I appreciated the help. I told him I was going to make peach crumble pie for dessert tonight. If he would do the dishes, I could finish it and get it in the fridge for later.

    We worked around each other while Maeve nursed another cup of tea. Once the kitchen was clean, the crumble pie was made and in the fridge for later, and Maeve felt more human, I went down to the shop while they got ready for the day. I sent Sean a text, thanking him for saving me last night and got back a kiss and a wink emoji. He asked how I felt and I responded that I felt better than his mom did. He laughed at that and said he would be by for dinner tonight. I told him I made dessert but I wasn't sure what was for dinner yet. I told him I would let Maeve know he was coming so I was sure it would be something good. He told me he would see me tonight and I said I would be there. Then I opened up the shop and got the cleaning supplies out.

The summer brought a lot of flies in Ireland, so Tom ran around with a fly swatter and I helped with the cleanup and disposal of his victims. Maeve manned the front counter and the phone. We helped customers throughout the day and Arthur came in to thank Maeve and me for visiting with Phyllis so often. He brought a large bunch of wildflowers for the shop before he went to spend the day with Phyllis. The perfume smell of the flowers was a little overwhelming so I took them upstairs and divided them into three vases. I scattered them about the store to help spread the fragrance. I thought they smelled good but Maeve was still a little green from last night so I didn't put any on the front counter.

It seemed like the whole town was coming into the store more often, trying to keep up on the gossip and the news or maybe just enjoying the weather. With tourists and buses and the bigger influx of the locals, it was a very busy day. We wound down the shop a little after seven in the evening because there were just so many people left at closing time. Maeve managed to steal away a few minutes and place a phone call to the Crow's Nest for dinner for the four of us. Sean had arrived at half-past-six and picked up our order on the way in. Three of us practically fell into our chairs. I did jump up to put the pie in the oven but was back in my chair with water to drink.

Sean laughed that Tom was the only one willing to drink with him that evening. We dug into our pizzas and salad. Maeve ordered all three pizzas they offered at the Crow's Nest and a couple of Caesar salads to split. The spicy chicken pizza was too much for me and the seafood pizza was really rich, but the veggie pizza was perfect, not that I didn't have a piece of each just to be sure, but the Caesar salad was the perfect pairing to eat between each slice. We ate practically in silence. I came up for air first. We were all starving. The timer went off for the pie and I got up to pull it out of the oven. Then I went back to my plate. With a full stomach and finally sitting down for the day, I could feel all the tension relax out of my muscles. It was hard to keep my eyes open.

Sean brought me out of my half-slumber when he asked if we could go for a walk to talk before dessert. Maeve handed Tom a dish towel and shooed us out of the kitchen. I went upstairs and changed my shoes. I wanted a little more cushion if I was going to be back on my feet.

I met Sean at the front door and he escorted me out, locking the door behind us. We walked a few minutes into the night and made our way to our little bridge. He sat on the County Mayo side and I sat on the County Galway side. We leaned slightly against each other. There was a slight breeze in the air.

He gave a deep sigh and quietly said, "Have you come back around to me then, love?"

I paused for a minute then whispered back, "it's going to hurt so much in September, but I can't push you out of my life any longer. I need you too much."

We sat for a long moment then he wrapped his arm around my waist and pulled me close. I reveled in his touch, missing him so much. I tried to hide a tear that ran down my cheek.

He squeezed me a little tighter and said, "Don't cry, love. The next month is going to be beautiful, no matter the weather. We will cross the bridge in September when we come to it."

We sat in silence, his arm around me, enjoying the cool summer breeze on our skin. I caught a chill and shivered a bit later. He rubbed my arm and then moved to get up. Holding out a hand, he helped me up. We walked hand in hand back to the book shop.

We stopped on the side of a building just before the street the shop was on. He leaned against the building and pulled me close. We kissed deeply, a welcome home kiss after a long time gone, the need and longing were evident in every move. His fingers ran through my hair, holding me so close we could have been one person. He pulled away first when Mr. Armstrong walked by slowly with his very old corgi. We pushed into the shadow, held our breath, and waited for him to pass.

With the mood broken, we exhaled quietly and walked slowly back to the book shop. Stopping to unlock the door, he whispered, "Come home with me." It wasn't a question. I smiled slightly but managed a, "not tonight."

He smiled as he sighed but let it pass. As I stepped through the door, I caught a glimpse of Maeve retreating into the kitchen. I smiled at Sean and told him that his mom knew we were back together. He said, "Aye, she will see me more again which will make her happy."

We walked up to the kitchen together; Tom and Maeve were in their room. I sat at the table. Sean pulled out the Jameson and a couple of glasses. He put an ice cube in one and poured the whiskey. He handed me the iced Jameson and sat next to me. We clinked our glasses together and said, "Slainte!"

Sean left after our drink, a piece of pie, and a long kiss goodnight. After I locked the door behind him, I walked slowly through the bookshelves. I noticed how very at ease I felt. As I walked up the staircase, I felt lighter. My life just felt right again.

Not having the energy to call my sister and explain my situation yet, I told myself I would call her and Mom tomorrow, and shot my dad a 'just checking in' text, then I changed for bed. Snuggled down in bed, I thought of Sean and about Phyllis.

29

A few days later, I woke up so tired but so excited for the day. I stayed up late the previous night finishing up the baby blanket for Molly's baby girl. It came out so cute and I managed a couple of matching headbands. *I hope they fit!* I wrapped them around a small butter tub like Maeve suggested. Mentally, I crossed my fingers.

Apparently, Maeve was excited too. I could hear her down in the kitchen already starting her prep for the party. She volunteered for the catering. By the time I had gotten dressed, packed my bag and the gift, and wandered down the spiral staircase, she had three kinds of cookies cooling on racks, frosting in the mixer, and the first batch of cupcakes coming out of the oven. There were brown bags sitting on a chair next to the stairs with Tom and Jayne written on them. Guessing that was a sign she didn't need my help, I didn't step into the kitchen. I picked up my bag just as Tom came out of the room. Wide eyed, he pointed at his bag, and I smiled. Timing it perfectly, he quickly walked past Maeve as she turned to put in another pan of cupcakes in the oven, he walked to me quickly. I handed him his bag and we walked down the stairs without a word.

Once we reached the shop on the ground floor, he said, "Best to leave her be. My Maeve has it all under control."

We opened up the shop and I helped get everything set up to leave Tom in charge for the afternoon while Maeve and I went to the baby shower. We set out new stock and pulled the Armstrong's most recent order from the back. Tom wouldn't let me dust so I was clean for the shower even though my dress was packed in a bag along with my gift, so it didn't get it dirty when I helped with set up, so I manned the front counter for the morning while he did the dusting in the fiction section.

There was enough food in our bags for breakfast and lunch so neither of us went back upstairs until around one o'clock when Maeve called for us. Walking upstairs into what smelled like a gourmet bakery, we saw Maeve happy as could be with all her masterpieces all boxed up and ready. She gave specific instructions on what order to take the boxes carefully down to the car since some contained warm food and some had food that could melt. I helped Tom get everything downstairs and then manned the shop while he loaded the car per her instructions. Maeve's hair was already in curlers, so she just had to pop in the shower, get cleaned up, pop out the rollers, and get dressed. She was deft at getting ready in a flash.

All the boxes were loaded when Maeve came down in a pretty pink and green dress. She kissed Tom goodbye and left a few instructions for him. I wished him luck. He laughed and said to keep the luck because I would need it more. Maeve walked out the front door and Tom cleared his throat.

I looked back and he whispered, "If one or two sweets could make it back in that bag of yours, they wouldn't be going to waste." I smiled and nodded, but as I turned around, Maeve was coming back in with a cupcake. She handed it to him and told him that was all he would be getting and not to ask anyone (she eyeballed me) to be bringing him sweets. As we left, he winked at me. *I would have to see what was left when we finished.*

We drove to Molly and Grant's house. They had a pretty back garden that the party was going to be held in with a low fence around it. When we arrived at the house, I couldn't help but think the house fit them. It was a semi-attached house, tan with dark brown trim and red brick. The front of the house was close to the street so there wasn't a large front garden, but they were near the corner of the street and there was a small community children's playground that wrapped around the corner of the green space. There were shade trees scattered around the area. Their back garden had a small gate that led to the playground. Maeve parked the car on the street near the playground and we got out, leaving all the boxes behind for the moment. We walked up to the front door, and before we could knock, Grant had the door open with a beaming smile. He was dressed in a pink button-down shirt and jeans. His dark chocolate complexion was a beautiful contrast to his light pink shirt. His face glowed with pride as he invited us in and gave us a quick tour of the house.

The house was perfect for a new baby. There were little pockets in each room where they started incorporating things for their new baby girl.

Molly was in the kitchen, arranging flowers in small mason jars. She greeted us both with a kiss on the cheek and then hugged Grant. She looked so cute in her matching pink dress next to Grant as he tucked one of her unruly red curls behind her ear. She was glowing and so happy the party was finally here.

Molly walked us outside and showed us the tables that Grant had set out and told us how she thought things should look. Then Maeve gently walked her to a chair and told her we could handle it. Grant handed Molly a glass of water, then the three of us got to work. We had it all set up in no time. Maeve was very direct with her instructions and Grant and I followed directions very well. Sandwiches, cookies, cupcakes, crisps, crackers and cheese, nuts, and candies all came out of Maeve's boxes.

About fifteen minutes before everyone was set to arrive, I snagged my bag out of the car and used the restroom to change. I put on a new dress I had gotten in town. It was blue with sage green and baby pink flowers on it. I had braided my hair that morning to give it a gentle wave. I carefully took out the braids and gave my head a flip to fluff it. I threw on a bit of blush, some eyeliner, and mascara. Taking a look in the mirror, I nodded, took a deep breath to prepare myself for the onslaught of people and took my bag back to the car.

The shower was on a Friday afternoon but everyone showed up in their Sunday best. All the ladies in town came, even Phyllis, who wasn't feeling well, showed up in a new dress. She said nothing would keep her from the party. Some of Molly and Grant's family from Cork and Dublin made the drive out. There were little cousins running around the garden and playing at the playground. Watchful mums and aunties kept an eye on them. It wasn't long before the garden was full of new dresses and trouser sets, and everyone was chatting about where they got their new frocks. Maeve settled Molly at the center table and then interrupted the chatter with an announcement that the food and drinks were available on the sideboard (a long table we set up to the left of the backdoor to the houses).

 I poured Prosecco and cranberry juice for all who wanted it and got Molly and Phyllis a glass of sparkling water with cranberry juice. Grant took the stage, as it were, and welcomed the guests. He toasted to his beautiful wife and new baby girl and followed up with quick goodbyes, leaving the shower to the ladies, as he put it.

 The eating and mingling lasted for just under an hour before Phyllis tired out and decided to head home. She said her goodbyes, Molly whispered something in her ear as she was leaving, and she beamed. She patted Molly's hand and told her she would be honored then, still beaming, she asked Arthur to take her home. When I asked Molly what she had said, she told me they were considering Phyllis's middle name for the baby and asked if it would be all right.

I smiled at Molly and then Maeve, with her infallible party plan timing, was asking for attention to start the first game.

We laughed and talked. We watched Molly open gift after gift. We played games and the more competitive ones were cutthroat about taboo words and collecting safety pins. I lost mine within five minutes which worked out well because I could say the word baby for the rest of the event without worrying if someone was going to take my safety pin.

Molly was so excited when she opened my gift. It made finishing it late last night worth it. I can't believe I kept pushing it off.

I helped Maeve keep the party going by rotating stock at the food table and refilled glasses as they emptied. When things started to wind down and the long-distance family said their goodbyes, Maeve and I helped shrink the party down inside the back garden. By the end of the night, there were just a few of us left re-looking at gifts. Maeve and I were the last to go as the party that fell out of Maeve's car was put back in, though this time, the boxes were lighter. Maeve drove us back home where we unloaded the car with Tom and Sean's help. We gathered up everything on the ground floor, and once the front door was locked, we all headed to the kitchen with everything. Leftovers from the party became dinner, as Maeve and I settled in at the table with a celebratory glass of whiskey.

The evening went by quietly. We talked about the party and about worries for Phyllis. Sean whispered that I was falling asleep sitting and it woke me from my daze. I dragged myself up from the table and headed toward the stairs. Sean was behind me. I could feel him there. He whispered that he wouldn't want me to fall on my way to bed. He walked me to his childhood bedroom and I kissed him soundly. He chuckled and told me he would see me soon. I shut the door and practically fell into bed.

30

A week later, on my next day off, I volunteered to go see Phyllis before I went to Ashford's library that afternoon. As I walked up the street with a new book and some sweets, something shifted in the air. A breeze blew by, but it felt different. Almost like I was hugged. I caught my breath and said Phyllis's name out loud. I started running towards her house. I got to the door, out of breath. I took two deep breaths to calm myself and knocked gently on the door. The nurse that answered the door had a handkerchief in her hand and a small tear in her eye. I searched her eyes and she nodded quietly, letting me into the small foyer.

"Is she...?" I asked.

She nodded slightly. "Arthur came last night because she was asking for him and we called. She slipped away just a few moments ago with him by her side. They had a good chat about old times last night and she rested peacefully after that, slipping away as gentle as a breeze."

I closed my eyes thinking of my breezy hug.

I thanked the nurse and told her I didn't want to disturb Arthur, but if he needed anything to call my cell or the book shop. Walking back to the book shop, I felt like a robot, mechanically saying hello to people and not really focused on anything.

I walked through the open door of the book shop and Maeve greeted the jingle of the bells from crouched behind the counter. Tom peeked over one of the bookshelves he was dusting and called to Maeve as he reached me. Tom caught me as I stumbled, and Maeve rushed over.

I managed to whisper the words, "she's gone," as they helped me to a chair behind the counter. Maeve cupped her hand over her mouth and Tom wiped a rogue tear from his cheek. I managed the quick story of my morning and what the nurse said, and Maeve took off upstairs to change clothes and call Arthur to help make arrangements for the funeral and the wake for him if he needed. Tom started to close up the shop but I told him I needed something to do to feel useful and that, if there were things he needed to do, I could watch the shop. He hugged me, made sure I was steady on the chair and went upstairs to see what Maeve needed help with.

The day passed in a blur. Tom and Maeve came and went to help with arrangements while I manned the shop and kept busy. News traveled fast so anyone who came in already knew which saved me from having to repeat it. At six o'clock, I closed up the shop and made the deposit. I walked upstairs and jumped into the shower, cold to the bone, even though it was a warm day. I let the heat soak into me until I was red. I got out and changed clothes, figuring I could offer help with things if there was still work to be done tonight. There was a knock on my bedroom door, Sean stood in the doorway. He held open his arms and caught me as I flew into them. I started sobbing; it was a big, ugly cry but it was cathartic. I'd held it in all day. Sean moved with me to the bed and held me, letting me get it all out. When I finally calmed down, he wiped tears from my face and offered me a handkerchief, I shook my head not wanting to mess it up and reached for the tissue box. I mopped up my messy face, noticing that he had cried a bit too, I hugged him back. We sat for a bit of time, not saying anything, just holding on to each other and offering support. Sean broke the silence when he asked if I was ready to go. I looked at him quizzically. He said the wake was tonight at Pat Cohan's. Most of the town had been there since it opened but the stories would start soon. I nodded but then I went to the bathroom to splash cool water on my face. I started to put on some makeup but Sean said, from the doorway, that no one would be wearing any. I nodded thoughtfully, grabbed a light sweater and a couple of boxes of tissues from the cupboard and we walked down to the pub.

The place was packed and there were instruments all around the room. The pints were pre-poured and sitting on the bar so we each took one and went to find a seat. I set the tissues next to me on the bench seat. There were cheese, fruit, and meat boards on every table and loaves of bread and butter too. Sean sat next to me and I asked him to fill me in on how this all worked.

He said a few of the townsfolk chipped in and bought all the pints and food you saw. If you wanted different food, you paid for that separately but the rest of the night, we would all be in here eating and drinking, telling stories, and singing her favorite songs.

I took a deep drink of my Guinness and snagged a piece of bread from the table. The music from the speakers quieted and Arthur stood near the bar. He thanked everyone for coming and raised his glass, "to Aunt Phyllis! May she rest in peace and not give God too much trouble up there!" The room erupted in murmurs of laughter, and everyone shouted, "to Phyllis!"

Stories and songs filled the night, Sean never left my side except to get us more to drink. Maeve was flitting about the place taking care of everyone. Tom seemed content at a table with the Armstrongs and Arthur. Occasionally, a voice would get loud enough for everyone to hear and the room would quiet for the story being told. A fresh-faced, but pink from crying, Molly walked in followed by Grant. She caught my eye and headed my way. I felt less self-conscious about not wearing any makeup when I saw her. We could sit fresh-faced together. I slid over a bit to give her room to sit. Sean walked up and stood with Grant in front of us. Molly and I talked about the baby. Grant grabbed a small stool from Jerry behind the bar and brought it over to Molly. He took a small pillow off the bench seat we were sitting on and then helped her prop up her feet. Molly groaned a little and complained about swelling in her ankles. It made me smile and I noticed my face was tight from crying.

"Sean was just filling me in on how things work," I said.

She patted my hand and said, "All the work is done for the night. Now we sit and relax and listen to the songs and stories." I glanced down at the great swell of her belly and watched it move. She grabbed my hand and placed it on her belly where it moved. I felt the baby move and kick. My eyes lit up. She laughed and said, "This little peanut has been extra active today. I think she likes the music." Grant crouched down and placed his hand where mine had been and lit up as well when he felt her move. He said, out loud to no one in particular, that this happened all the time, but he was still so fascinated by it.

Once the baby settled again, Grant stood back up. Sean asked for drink orders. I asked for another Guinness, Molly asked for a club soda with cranberry juice—her new favorite drink. Grant threw an arm over Sean's shoulder and said he would buy this round as they walked to the bar together. Molly and I sat back and listened to the music. It came from all around. Instruments were in every corner of the room. Some songs were happy and lively, and others, sad and somber. The guys came back to the table a few songs later, having stopped a couple of times to chat with people as they passed. I accepted my drink and clinked glasses with each of them.

I asked Sean if I should be helping Maeve. He told me to look at her.

"Have you ever seen her more in her element than when she is helping others?" I nodded at him and then helped Molly get some food from the table. I made us both a napkin full of items from the charcuterie boards on the table so she didn't have to lean forward and drop her feet.

We spent most of the evening that way, slightly scooting one way or the other to accommodate more people. Molly and I decided we needed more food than just the snacks available, and when Maeve came by to check on her, Molly asked if we could get a bowl of soup each. I told Maeve that I could go order it from the bar and she shook her head and gestured for me to stay seated. She walked over to Jerry and told him what we wanted. Jerry looked up at us and I gestured to him that it could go on my tab. He nodded his head. In no time at all, two steaming bowls of blended veggie soup with bread and butter were sitting in front of us. We tucked in, getting about halfway through each before we gave in. Molly set her bowl on the table; it had been resting on a towel on her belly and told Grant to have the rest. I asked Sean if he wanted the rest of mine. They sat down their drinks and finished off the soup.

There were more stories from Phyllis's life and songs of old. Molly called it quits at half-past-eleven just after the song, *The Parting Glass*. Grant took her home after we said our goodnights. Sean reclaimed his spot next to me and we settled in for a few more hours. Around half-past-two in the morning, I started to fall asleep. Things had wound down a bit, but the music was still going. Arthur stood up at the bar, swaying slightly.

"Thank you all for coming. Please enjoy this early morning and get home safe when you go. I will see you all at the funeral." He raised the last of his drink and finished it off. A few men helped him stumble out the door. I assumed he was going back to Phyllis's house.

Not long after, Sean patted my leg and asked if I was ready to go. I nodded sleepily and we went around the room and said our good nights to everyone. Maeve said they were going to open the book shop in the afternoon so we could sleep in.

Sean walked me outside and pulled me close. "May I spend the night with you?" I asked without even thinking. It just felt right. It caught him slightly off-guard, but he recovered quickly and gave me a hug. I walked hand and hand with him to the book shop to get some clothes. Quickly packing an overnight bag, I left Maeve a note and we headed to his house. I cuddled close to him in the lorry as we drove in silence. When we arrived, I expected things to be awkward, but everything felt so right. He quickly grabbed my bag from the bed of the lorry and opened my door. We walked to the door hand in hand. He handed me a single key. I unlocked the door. Setting everything down in the hall, we walked to the kitchen. He asked if he could get me anything. Shaking my head, no, I walked to the cupboards and pulled out the bottle of Jameson I knew would be there.

I smiled and said, "How about I get us a night cap?" He reached for some glasses and I grabbed a few ice cubes for my drink. I poured the whiskey over the ice in my glass and neatly into his glass. We clinked glasses together and both took a sip. We visibly relaxed slightly as the cool liquid warmed as it went down.

In one movement, the glass was out of my hand and I was in his arms. He tried to carry me and kiss me as he walked down the hall but he managed to clip my foot on the corner. He stumbled a couple of steps while I hung on for dear life. He managed to stay upright and was trying to apologize while I was laughing. He set me down gently and I played up a large limp, as I continued down the hall. He tried to scoop me up again and I took off running to the bedroom, forgetting all about my hurt foot. I dove onto the bed and he landed next to me a second later. He wrapped me in his arms, holding me still. He asked if he hurt me and I told him I was fine. I kissed his nose. He kissed me back softly and then slowly deepened the kiss. I softly purred and he deepened it more, moving his hand over me. We took our time removing one piece of clothing at a time from each other. Kissing every inch of newly exposed skin. When we ran out of clothing, he slid himself off the edge of the bed pulling me to him. Gently parting my legs, he ran his lips and tongue down the inside of my thigh until he reached my warm center. He slowly teased me until I gasped then he buried his face between my thighs.

I gasped again and then relaxed as he patiently worked me towards a climax. His expert tongue coaxing and teasing soft cries from me, all while I arched and moaned for more. My muscles locked as he held me in place, not letting me get away. I cried out in ecstasy, tumbling over the edge. He held me tight as my climax quaked through me. I felt my body throb against his mouth. He moaned softly as if my flavor changed to something more delicious. He waited for the last dregs of my climax to quiet. Contently smiling as he climbed on top of me.

I kissed him deeply, never wanting this to end. I heard the wrapper of a condom and pulled back to let him work. He had it on in seconds and was back to kissing me. I parted my legs more, though they were slightly weak, and he entered my soft, hot center. In a rhythm so exquisite, we kissed and coaxed and teased until he couldn't take it any more. My hips rose to match his rhythm. I held him tightly as he peaked hard and fast. I let his quaking slow down. He pressed his forehead to mine and breathlessly kissed me. We rolled to the side and softly kissed some more.

I kissed him on the nose and said, "I won." He smirked and raised an eyebrow.

"If I'm not mistaken, I think we are tied." We laughed and I turned over to curl up in his arms.

31

The funeral was a full Catholic mass. I had to reach way into the depths of my memory from catechism classes to hope I was doing things correctly. Sean was by my side and I found myself copying him for most of the funeral. I was more worried about messing up than paying attention to what I was actually there for. We moved from the church to the graveside and I gave myself some time to say goodbye to Phyllis in my head. I didn't know her very long but she had become another grandma to me and a friend. We were all given flowers to lay on her casket. I had written her a letter while I covered the shop yesterday and tied it to the flower. When it was my turn, I laid it carefully on the casket. The flower petals wriggled in the breeze sending out their beautiful fragrance. Sean held my hand as they lowered the casket into the ground. Arthur wept softly in the front row, surrounded by his small family. The priest thanked everyone for coming and extended an invitation back to Phyllis's house for refreshments.

It wasn't the wake all over again. It was pastries from a local shop with tea and coffee. Beers and wine were available for those who wanted but the gathering was more subdued. Phyllis's house had been cleaned and photos of her and her family had been added around the house. Someone had found all her class photos from when she was a teacher and put them in an album on the table. I flipped through, watching her get younger with each page. I found Sean's class. He was standing next to her on a riser, holding her hand. He whispered that he wouldn't stay still for the photo so she rearranged the children and made him stand next to her. I snapped a picture of the two of them with my phone and texted it to him and Maeve. I wasn't the only one taking photos of photos. There were soft conversations about photos and the memories they recalled happening all around us. I did my best to stay out of the way and helped with refreshments, in need of distraction.

The gathering wound down slowly. Visitors trickled out after stories had been told and retold. Sean and I stayed until the end with several people to help clean up. Tom was in the kitchen starting the dishes as we all took turns bringing in all the dirty dishes from around the house. Once Maeve was satisfied with the state of the house, she shooed us out and let Arthur and his family have the rest of the evening.

We walked back to The Turning Page quietly. The town as a whole felt sad. Maeve asked if we wanted to have dinner. I threw out the idea of a charcuterie board, knowing we had a bunch of leftovers that would work for it and we didn't have to do any cooking. Sean and Tom agreed. Sean and I stopped at the convenience store at the petrol station to pick up a couple of bottles of wine and told Maeve and Tom we would be along soon. They waved at us and continued on to the shop. Sean scooped me up in a big hug, just outside the store doors, and held me tight for a few minutes. He whispered something I couldn't hear and he wouldn't repeat it when I asked. He took a deep breath and released me. He shook his head with a soft chuckle and asked me what kind of wine I wanted. I started to question him further but something inside said to let it go for now, so I said something dry and white, maybe a Sauvignon Blanc. He nodded his head, took my hand and we walked into the store and went to the wine aisle.

We got to The Turning Page a short time later, Maeve had already had the fridge cleaned out and had it all on the table. We poured the wine and ended the night with stories from each of us about Phyllis. Sean came upstairs with me for the night.

32

In the week that followed, I stayed busy at the shop; we all did, not wanting to have time to ourselves to think about Phyllis. I couldn't bring myself to remove her name that was taped to the basket in the stockroom yet. The month of July came to an end and we all took a deep breath.

August the first was a sunny day; no rain in the forecast and the air seemed lighter. I woke up alone, though Sean hadn't been gone long. It was my day off but he had to work. I stretched and yawned in bed and took a minute to get myself moving. It was still early but I wanted time at the library to finish *The Last September* and maybe find a new book before I went hiking after lunch. I threw on some comfy workout wear and packed my backpack with a raincoat and umbrella, just in case, and put my hair in two French braids, I headed down the stairs and could hear Tom and Maeve just getting up. I made a sandwich and packed up snacks for the day. I had put the kettle on to boil so when Maeve came over and saw it was ready, she squeezed my arm and whispered, "Bless you!" I told them both to have a great day and to text if they needed anything. I would be back in time for dinner.

Maeve waved goodbye and Tom raised his mug of tea. I locked up the shop and walked towards the abbey. The town was still quiet, just a few kegs of beer that had been deposited outside the pub and restaurant were proof that I wasn't the first one up today.

The green path to the castle was more vibrant as the sun started to peek through the trees. The birds sang their morning songs and I couldn't help but feel lighter. Today was going to be a good day, you could feel it in the air.

I met Shelly at the door as she unlocked the library. She greeted me with a silent nod and a smile. She let me in first and the two of us turned on lamps that were scattered around the room. The library had north-facing windows so there was never direct sunlight on the books, so you always needed the lamps to read by.

Once all the lamps were on, Shelly went to her desk and I went to what had become my corner of the library to set up my space. I pulled out my phone and found the page number I had stopped at the last time I came to read, then I put on a pair of gloves and retrieved the book from the shelf. I set it in the cradle and snuggled into the chair for the morning.

About three hours later, I turned the last page, took one deep breath, and closed the book. I took a minute to collect my thoughts about the book, then picked it up and placed it gently on the shelf. It was an excellent book. I cleaned up my area and decided against searching for a new book right away. I had the book I bought from the airport, which was also almost finished, and my e-reader.

Also, I needed time to process the many adventures of Lois Farquar.

I placed the cradle over by Shelly's desk, thanked her for the book recommendation and waved goodbye. With my backpack slung over my shoulder, I went to go find a spot out on the grass to have my lunch. When I stepped outside, I felt my phone buzzing. Four text messages came in all at once. They were from Maeve. I must have lost signal in the library.

I opened the thread and read quickly through the long texts. She must have talked texted instead of typed because they weren't making much sense but what I could gather was that Molly was at the hospital having the baby. I sent her a text back telling her I just got all her messages and that I was on my way back.

Sean came around the corner in the golf cart and stopped. He said his mom was trying to get a hold of me. I held up my phone and told him I just got her messages, and I texted her back. He said she was waiting for me if I wanted to join her and go see the baby at the hospital. He said he could take me in the golf cart as far as the abbey to save me some of the walk. I jumped on the cart, and on the quick drive, I shared my sandwich with him. I left him the rest of my lunch and kissed him goodbye. I told him I would see him tonight. He said he would work out dinner with his dad and to run, Mom was waiting.

I made it back to the shop just as Maeve was coming down the stairs, giving instructions to Tom that he already knew but it made her feel better to say them. When she saw me, she smiled.

"Are you ready to go meet the new baby?" I asked if she had arrived yet and Maeve said she got a text an hour ago that Renae Elizabeth Campbell was born at ten-twenty-seven that morning. Renae was Phyllis's middle name, she explained.

Maeve had a bouquet of flowers and a small gift bag in one hand and her purse and keys in the other. We went to the car and headed out to Sacred Heart Hospital, about forty minutes away. On the drive, I wondered out loud how Molly made it to the hospital in time. Maeve said that she went to the hospital last night with labor pains, and as she walked through the doors of the hospital, her water broke. Eight hours of labor and Miss Renae was here, two weeks early. My mind boggled at the thought of eight hours of labor. My mom told the stories of our births to Sam and me on every birthday. She was in labor for forty-five minutes with me and only three hours with Sam. It never occurred to me that it would go much longer than that. Maeve said she was in labor for twenty hours with Sean. My eyes got even wider and she laughed. She said she knew from the very first day that Sean was going to be stubborn. We both laughed. I didn't say it out loud but Sean got the stubbornness from her.

We got to the hospital and I stayed a little behind Maeve as she spoke in English and Irish to the counter staff. She handed me a visitor pass and repeated the directions to the nursery.

Down a long hall, there was a large window. We peeked inside and there were rows of babies in clear plastic bassinets. All the babies were wrapped in blankets with tiny beanies on their heads. Some were asleep while others were crying and wiggling. I caught the eye of a nurse who pointed to a small intercom on the wall. I walked over and pressed the button. She asked what the last name of the baby we were there to see was, I said Campbell. She nodded and walked over to a bassinet, scooped up a tiny bundle, and walked over to the window. Maeve and I oohed and aahed over the tiny person. She was so pretty for an infant. She had light mocha skin that was smooth and soft-looking. When Sam was born, she was speckled pink and red with what my mom called stork bites and she had little bumps all over her face. Renae was perfect. Maeve gestured to the nurse to remove the beanie on her head. The nurse complied, and in one quick swoop, a tiny head with medium reddish-brown swirls emerged. They looked wet, like they had put baby oil on them and were all pressed flat to her tiny head. We both swooned a little. She was so perfect.

We nodded and thanked the nurse, waving goodbye, she put Renae back in her bassinet. Maeve headed down the hall further and went through a doorway. Then went three doors down and walked in. I followed behind. Grant was just helping Molly back into bed. Maeve set down the flowers and hugged them both. I said congratulations and asked Molly how she was feeling. She said she was tired but in good spirits. She asked if we got to see Renae in the nursery yet. I smiled and nodded as Maeve told her how beautiful she was. Grant said they both had a chance to hold her right away but they took her to the nursery for a bath. She should be coming back soon if we wanted to stay and hold her. Maeve and I beamed with joy. Nurses came to check on Molly and gave the all-clear to have the baby brought back. Moments later, Renae was in Maeve's arms. We sat for a bit while Maeve unwrapped the baby, counted fingers and toes, checked her from her head to her toes, then wrapped her back up. Molly laughed and said they both did the same thing when they held her for the first time.

After a bit of time, Maeve reluctantly relinquished the baby to me. Babies aren't completely foreign to me but it had been a while. Maeve tucked Renae into my waiting arms. She was so tiny and light.

"Just over six-and-a-half pounds.", said Grant.

"Six pounds, ten ounces, not bad for two weeks early," corrected Molly as she took off Renae's beanie and ran her fingers through her curls. "She got her daddy's curls but my hair color came through a bit too."

After a few more oohs and aahs, Molly and Grant's family started to arrive so it was time for us to leave. I handed the baby to Grant and I hugged Molly gently goodbye. On the drive back to Cong, Maeve and I talked about the baby and her pregnancy with Sean. Then we wondered what the boys decided to do for dinner. I sent Sean a text letting him know we were on our way back. He said dinner would be ready when we arrived. We finished the drive, making it back in time to help close the shop. Sean yelled down from the kitchen that he was just finishing up dinner. Tom did the deposit and Maeve and I tidied the store. We walked upstairs together when everyone was finished. Sean had ordered dinner from the castle. It was the same meal we ate on our first date, the night on the boat with Seamus. Sean had the whole table set and had served everyone already. He opened a couple of bottles of red wine and poured everyone a glass as we sat down.

We spent the evening telling them all about the baby. The ladies did the cleanup then I walked Sean out to his lorry and kissed him goodnight. We lingered for a bit, not wanting a great day to end but he had to be at work early in the morning so just one more goodnight kiss and a lingering hug and he was on his way home. On my way back into the shop, I decided to take some time that evening and call home. I went upstairs and called my mom first. She was doing well; she had to take Lady to the vet's office last week. Lady liked to play in the foxtails and she got one in her ear Mom couldn't get out. Mom filled me in on all the family gossip I had missed that week and I told her about the funeral and the new baby.

We ended our call with her telling me to call my sister. She'd been in a state because of the wedding. I placed that call next. Sam liked video-calls so she can see me and make faces at me. She asked about my week and I filled her in on all that happened. Then she started with the wedding details. I told her she had time but she was beyond hearing that. We talked about venues, flowers, cake flavors, and guests. She was on a roll. The clock in my room said half-past-eleven when I had to cut her off. I told her I would call her later that week and we could talk more but I needed to go to bed. She blew me a kiss and said goodnight. I sent a quick 'thinking of you' text to my dad, then my head hit the pillow and I was out.

33

The whole week following the birth of Renae was helping Tom and Maeve get ready for their three-week trip to the Faroe Islands. Extra supplies and stock were ordered for the shop and I was able to squeeze in one last day off the day before they left.

Sean and I had the day off together; he'd promised me a hawk walk with Fern now that the babies were growing and had been moved to another pen. Sean needed to take her out to see if she was ready for customers.

I had spent the night at his house and we drank way too much wine that night so we slept in for most of the morning. It was half-past-ten in the morning when I stirred in his arms. He tightened his arms around me and I heard a soft groan. I licked his lower lip and watched his smile and felt something else grow. I ran my hand down his chest, sliding all the way down to his thigh and back up. He arched his back when I took hold of him. I slid my body down his easily enough since we weren't wearing any clothes. I picked up a condom off the nightstand and put it on him. I had gotten really good at doing that quickly. I settled myself on him. He groaned as he entered me. I leaned down to kiss him and whispered, good morning, as I started to move up and down. He held onto my hip and back and rolled us over, continuing the rhythm I had started. I tightened and released around him with the rhythm we were creating, bringing him to his climax, he held me tight. When he relaxed a bit, I brought my lips to the tip of his nose, kissed it quickly and announced that I had won. He growled at me and said the day was still young. I told him there was always later but we had plans. I squirmed my way out from under him and headed to the shower.

It was lunchtime by the time we were ready to face the world. We packed up the lorry after we finished eating and headed to the castle. George was in the office when we arrived. I gave him a hug as he came around the counter.

"Would you look at the two of you! You're a right smart-looking couple, you are!" George exclaimed. I thanked him and kissed him on the cheek. He blushed a bit and shooed us out of the office. He told Sean that Fiona and Fergus had gone for a trial run in the large pen yesterday after he had left. Fiona did well and returned to the glove right away but Fergus took extra coaxing to get him back.

"Fern should be proud of her wee offspring, she should." George said.

We went down the walkway and I stopped at the pen that used to have Fern and the babies in it. Sean told me that was the hatching pen and that Fern was moved just down the way. It was smaller than the hatching pen but there was lots of room for her. The pen next to her had the twins. They wouldn't be separated for some time yet, Sean explained. I took some chicken bits and placed them in a pouch, hooking it to my belt loop, then grabbed a glove. Sean did the same and then he opened the door to Fern's pen and stepped inside. Fern hopped onto Sean's glove and he stepped out of the enclosure. I put a small bit of chicken on my glove and held it out to her. She transferred gently over to my glove. Sean reminded me that Fern was not like Archimedes. She was not a cuddler.

Sean decided to take out Fiona to see how she would do without her brother around and with Mom showing her what to do. We walked out to a small grass area on the side of the aviary. Sean nodded his head for me to release Fern. I let go of her lead and lifted my arm slightly. Fern fluffed up her feathers and expanded her wings. She launched from my arm and soared into the sky. It was breathtaking.

After about five minutes as Fern circled the area, he said, "Let's see how Fiona does." He dropped her lead and raised his arm. She spread her wings and launched into the air just like Fern, though she was smaller. She soared through the sky around Fern, like they were playing. He let them play for a few minutes, then said we should try to bring them back. He let out a whistle signaling to Fern to come back. We both placed chicken on our gloves. Fern flew down toward me and circled once, before she landed gently on my wrist, enjoying her treat. Fiona took a little more coaxing. Fern seemed to understand, and just before Sean could whistle again, she let out a cry. Fiona's flight changed directions and she glided down to Sean's glove. He chuckled and offered some extra chicken bits to Fern as a thank you.

Sean took Fiona's lead in hand and said it was a great try, but if we want to take Fern into the forest, then little Fiona would need to go back first. We walked back and put Fiona in her pen and then headed out. Sean looked around and said to let Fern loose as we walked across the well-tended grounds of Ashford. There were plenty of visitors at the castle that afternoon and Fern received a lot of notice. A young couple pointed her out to their three young children. The oldest, a boy of about five, caught sight of Fern and clapped his hands.

Just as we got to the edge of the forest, Sean let out a whistle and I raised my arm after placing chicken on my glove. Fern soared in the sky in one single loop and then landed gracefully on my wrist. We went into the forest, walking through the trees. There were plenty of people out for hikes on the trail. Fern got lots of attention. I kept a hold of her lead but held her so people could get a good look. We had a few people who decided to follow us. About ten minutes into the hike, we found an open area where the trees had thinned. I let go of Fern's lead, lifted my arm, and let her launch into the air. The couple of people that stayed with us on the hike were audible in their amazement. It really was extraordinary to watch her fly. Much different from Archimedes; she was sleeker and faster. She zipped around the area, then landed on a branch in a distant tree, watching as Sean and I wandered around the opening in the forest. The sky was so blue with big puffy clouds scattered around. Sean held my hand as we walked. Fern stayed perched in the tree so the people that followed us into the forest had moved on. I asked if he would be staying with me while his parents were on vacation. He said he would if I wanted him to stay. I told him I would and that I was done trying to sort it out in my head. Phyllis said to let go so I had. I just liked spending time with him, and if I never saw him again after I went home, I would have wonderful memories to think back on, but I also hoped we could be together again someday. He squeezed my hand and told me that everything would work out, he had not yet figured out how, but it would, so, for now, we were just going to enjoy what time we had together. I nodded my head.

Meanwhile, Fern was enjoying her time, skipping from branch to branch, soaring in the air searching for food. Every time she launched from a branch and circled the area, I found myself astonished by her beauty. Sean and I fantasized about how things would be If I didn't have to go back to California. We talked of places we could go together and things we would do, moving my stuff into his house, finding a job somewhere in Cong, maybe seeing if I could stay on at the bookshop. We thought of all the things that could be and it all sounded so wonderful. I started to think that it could just be real, it might just happen, though I didn't know how.

A little while later, Sean decided it was time to go in so he whistled once for Fern and she, again, landed gently on my arm. I gave her several pieces of chicken bits as we walked back through the forest and back to the aviary. We put Fern back in her pen and went back to the office to say goodbye to George. He looked a little frazzled when we walked in, there were several customers in the lobby and the phone was ringing.

He said, "I don't know what you two did but you stirred something in the guests! We are selling out on hawk walks for weeks!" Sean laughed and said that taking Fern out must've been good for business and he jumped behind the counter to help George with customers while I grabbed the phone. After the rush of people and the phone calls stopped, we sat back in the lobby and talked about ideas for advertising by taking the hawks out on the grounds of Ashford, maybe during lunchtime when everyone was out on a sunny day having lunch on the grounds.

A short time later, Sean and I left the office and headed to Cong for the evening. Maeve was at the ready with dinner and dessert. We had picked up a few bottles of wine and a dessert port to go with the meal. Maeve had cooked up a storm, as per usual, and she spent most of the day meal-prepping for Sean and me for the first couple of weeks that they would be gone. I told her I could handle the rest. She said there were frozen meals she had prepped last week in the freezer if I needed them.

After dinner, Maeve and Tom went to their room early to finish packing and to get ready to leave in the morning. They found cheaper flights out of Dublin so Sean had taken the day off to take them in the morning. Sean and I cleaned up the kitchen and then headed upstairs, where we hung out on the little couch and he put on a football game until I called it a night and we went to bed. That night I had vivid dreams about what could be if I stayed.

34

The next morning was a whirlwind, we all got up after Sean wanted to cuddle in bed longer and we got everything packed and ready for them to take off. Once Sean was on his way with his parents to Dublin International Airport, I settled in for my three weeks alone at the shop. I took several days' worth of lunches down to the small fridge behind the register. I made sure I had enough water to get me through the days as well. I grabbed a quick bite to eat for breakfast and then went down to open the shop. I opened the front door and propped it open; it was going to be a beautiful blue-sky day. There was a small chance of rain in the afternoon, but the sun should shine through before the evening.

Sean's drive should take him about four hours to get to Dublin with Maeve and Tom in the car. Then he had to get them unloaded and head back. It should take him just over three hours to get back since Maeve wouldn't be in the car telling him to slow down. He arrived about half-past-four in the afternoon, just as the Armstrongs were leaving with their weekly purchases. They stopped and chatted with him while I tidied up the register area after a busy day at the shop. They said goodbye and Sean helped me until closing. We finished out the evening with him telling me the story of his trip across the country with his parents and how he was going to have to do it again in three weeks when they returned, and I told him of all the things that happened at the shop.

For the rest of the week, we fell into a comfortable pattern; we would get up in the morning and have breakfast together, he would head off to work and I would go down to the shop, we would text back and forth throughout the day, and then he would come back at dinner time, help me close the shop, then we would tell each other about our day over dinner and a glass of wine or Jameson. In the evenings, we would hang out together and watch TV or I would call home, then we would head to bed, making love and falling asleep in each other's arms.

35

One night on a phone call to my sister, Sam was in tears. She and Mom had gotten into a fight over the guest list for the wedding. Sam wanted a big wedding but she didn't necessarily want hundreds of people there, especially people she didn't know. Sam rattled off a list of names she didn't know that Mom had put on her list for the wedding. People Mom grew up with but hadn't talked to in years. Some of them I didn't know either. So, playing the mediator, I called our mother and tried to smooth things over. All the while, Sean was holding my hand, nodding, or shaking his head as necessary, but not saying a word. I told my mom that it was Sam's wedding and she shouldn't have to invite or pay for a dinner for people she didn't know existed. Mom and I went through each person on the list Sam gave me. She told me who they were and why they needed to be there. We negotiated the list and dwindled it down to just a few people instead of the forty-five she had originally wanted, people that Sam might remember if I told her a story or two. I called Sam back and she was calmer and happy that she could take over forty names off her list. I told her a few stories from when we were growing up that she might remember about the few names Mom was being stubborn about, but at least I knew them. Sam allowed them to remain and said she was sitting all of them at the table with Mom. I reminded her that Mom would be sitting at the table near the front and said she should put them in the back since she didn't know them that well. Once I hung up the phone with Sam, Sean scooped me up into his arms and whispered, "Thank goodness I don't have siblings," in my ear.

36

Two weeks flew by in a flash without any breaks and hardly any sleep, thanks to our appetite for fun in the bedroom. Sean had a day off and he let me sleep in one morning while he opened the shop for me. I woke up around ten in the morning, got dressed, and headed down to the kitchen to get some tea and toast. I heard the bell jingle as a customer walked through the door and I heard Sean exclaim, "Oh my days, would you look at her!" I peeked out over the railing and saw that the Campbells had come in with Renae. I set down my tea and flew down the stairs to greet them.

    I engulfed Molly in a hug but I remembered at the last minute to be gentle. She returned the hug with a force that told me I wouldn't hurt her. I said hello to Grant over Molly's shoulder. Sean was crouched over the baby in the stroller. Her little hand was wrapped around his pinky finger. Renae was awake and looking around. Though, it wasn't long before her tiny mouth formed an O as she gave the tiniest yawn. Grant started to rock the stroller a little and she fell asleep quickly.

Molly laughed quietly and whispered, "That's all she does for now." Then she asked if I wanted to hold her. I told her I didn't want to wake her but Molly said she probably won't even stir. Molly unbuckled her out of her car seat and scooped her up. She kissed her on the cheek and then handed her to me.

Renae was just over two-weeks-old and all dressed up in the tiniest outfit I had ever seen. Soft cream lace and pink ribbons adorned her tiny sundress and bloomers. She had a matching bonnet and booties. Grant told Sean that this was her first outing. Molly was going stir-crazy, so they decided to come and get the baby new children's books for her bookshelf. They gestured towards the children's section and I cautiously followed. The two of them looked around while I held the perfect sleeping baby in my arms. Sean stayed near the front of the store but he could see me with Renae. He had a sly grin on his face for a second and then caught me looking at him. He smiled wide and winked at me. I found myself rocking from side to side automatically, as if when someone puts a baby in your arms your body knows that is what you do.

Molly and Grant were comparing books so I looked down at the infant in my arms. I remembered seeing pictures of myself just five-years-old holding Sam. She wasn't the last baby I ever held but she definitely was the smallest. Sam was premature, only five pounds and one ounce, but holding Renae now, she seemed like the smallest baby in the world.

Once Molly and Grant made the decision to get all of the books they looked at, we headed back to the register. I asked Sean if he wanted to hold her. He looked at me, face pale, eyes wide and said she was too small, he might drop her. Molly set the books on the counter and scooped Renae out of my hands telling him he would do just fine. Molly walked around the back of the register and told him to sit on the stool. He complied but tried to tell her he was good, but she heard none of it. She told him to make a cradle with his arms and he did. Then she laid Renae down in the crook of his elbow. She moved his hands slightly so he had a stable hold of her and placed her hands on her hips and said, "There! That's not so bad, is it?" Sean looked slightly uncomfortable and Grant laughed at him. He told him he would get used to it. Sean said he liked babies when they were less fragile. When they could play back and could tell him what they wanted.

Molly laughed and told him that wasn't a baby, it was a toddler. Molly had grown up with four siblings and a bunch of cousins, so babies weren't new to her. The pregnancy part was new, but now that Renae was here, she was in her element. Sean stayed completely still and wouldn't move a muscle. I told him I would save him and scooped Renae out of his arms. I nodded at the stack of books and he rang them up while I got in one last cuddle. Molly paid for the purchase while I handed Grant the baby to put back in her car seat. She slept through everything, that is, until Daddy tried to buckle her in her seat. Renae started to cry the smallest, sweetest infant cry. Grant panicked a little and started to rock the stroller. Molly said it was almost time for her to eat again. Grant shushed and soothed the baby and started pacing while pushing the stroller back and forth. Molly hugged me goodbye and Grant waved as he walked outside with the baby. The baby quieted as they walked back down the street.

I wrapped my arms around Sean's neck and had to make fun of him for being afraid of a brand-new baby. He started to defend himself and then told me to piss off. I laughed, jumped back from his pretend push, grabbed a duster and went to the non-fiction section to dust, laughing on my way.

The rest of the day was fairly quiet so I went around and cleaned the books on the top shelves, something that was usually Tom's job, but since he wasn't here and it had been a couple of weeks, I figured I would take care of it since Sean could run the front counter.

We closed the shop after saying goodbye to a dad and his daughter. She was around ten-years-old, adorable in her glasses and overall skirt and very specific in her request for science books. She settled on a book that had at-home science experiments in it.

We closed up and I did the deposit. Then Sean threw a cleaning cloth at me. I caught it before it hit me. He offered dinner at the pub. I threw the cloth back at him and agreed. We closed up the shop behind us and walked slowly to the pub. He held my hand and I wrapped myself around his arm. Then he let go, lifted his arm over my head and around my shoulder, kissing me on the head.

We walked into Pat Cohan's and waved at Jerry. He pointed us to an open table and held up two fingers. We nodded on our way by, and within a few minutes, two Guinnesses were set down in front of us. I watched as mine settled, separating the black beer from its creamy head. The first sip was always the best. Sean and I ordered dinner; soup of the day and brown bread and butter. We relaxed into our meal and our beers. It had been a long two weeks. One more left before Tom and Maeve came home.

That week, we had a visit from Arthur because, as he put it, "Old habits… " I told him he was always welcome. I let him wander the shop for a bit then, as he walked by me, not quite himself, I mentioned the baby coming out to visit the shop last week. He hadn't been around for the news. I told him the baby's name (with the less common spelling of Renae just like Phyllis's middle name) and he perked up. I hoped at some point he got to meet her. He went to the children's section and asked for help picking out a book they hadn't bought. He bought it and asked if I would save it for them for the next time they came in. I told him I would put it in the back. I gave him a slip of paper and a pen so he could write a small note and slid it inside the book. I placed a sticky note on it with the information and set it aside to put in The Campbell's basket.

Arthur left looking like he felt a little lighter. I hoped time would help him get through. The rest of the week passed quietly, though we did have a few buses of tourists bustling through the streets and I had my best sales day that week.

Sean worked long days that week, making up some time so he could take tomorrow off to make the drive to Dublin to get his parents from the airport. I closed up the shop a little late that evening, made the deposit, and went upstairs to make dinner.

I only had a couple of weeks left before I flew home and it was our last night alone in the shop. We had pot roast yesterday, so I made shredded beef tacos with the leftovers. When Sean arrived, I had a Jameson and ginger ale in hand for him and we ate and talked about our days.

That evening love-making was tender and slow. We both knew the end was coming but neither of us said anything out loud.

37

The next morning, the rain poured outside. Sean made me some tea while I made breakfast, then he helped me get the shop open and I kissed him goodbye. It was going to take about eight-and-a-half hours for him to get to Dublin, find his parents at the airport, take them to eat, then head back.

The day started out quietly. I was putting out some extra stock near the register when my cell phone rang. It was Sam's ringtone. I rushed around the counter to get my phone from behind the register. It was way too early in the morning for Sam to be awake. She was hysterical when I answered. I tried to calm her down. Jake took the phone from her and told me our dad had a fall at work. He was alive but unconscious. They took him to the hospital nearby his work. Sam choked out that I had to come home right away, they didn't know if he was going to wake up. I told her I would check flights and see what I could do. I would call them back.

I logged on to the airline's website and found a flight from Shannon to LAX with a layover in Seattle. I could be home in about nineteen hours. I would have to leave in two hours to get to Shannon in time for the flight. I called

Maeve and left her a voicemail. She was still in the air. I told her I was sorry but I had to close the shop early, my dad fell at work and I needed to fly home. I told her he was not conscious and they weren't sure if he was going to wake up. I continued that I'd found a flight out of Shannon and I was going to see if Grant could take me to the airport. I asked her to please tell Sean I would call him when I could. I hung up the phone and called Grant. Molly answered the phone.

I told her what had happened and she said, "Of course, Grant can take you. I'll send him right now."

I made a sign for the door and locked it up. I ran upstairs to pack while I called Sam back. She answered on the first ring. I told her when my flight would leave and when I should land at LAX. She told me she and Jake would be there to pick me up. I made it to my room breathless. I grabbed randomly at my clothes and threw them in my bag. I loaded up my backpack with my electronics, passport and headphones for the flight. I was downstairs waiting for Grant in about twenty minutes.

I sent Sean a text, telling him what happened and what my plan was. He called me right away. He told me he wasn't quite halfway to Dublin and he was turning around so he would meet me at Shannon Airport. I told him when my flight was scheduled to take off and that I didn't think he could get there on time safely.

I said, "Maybe it's better this way and what about your parents? We are supposed to part as friends, remember?

Deep down we knew it would end. I would eventually have to go home."

He said, "My parents can take the train from Dublin. It's not over!" He tried to argue but heard me cry softly and stopped. Grant pulled up and I told Sean I had to go. He told me he loved me with vehemence and said he was going to see me at Shannon, that I wasn't leaving without a kiss. I told him to please be careful but I wouldn't be able to wait for him, I had to be on that plane. I told him I loved him too and I would call him once I figured out what was going on at home. I hung up before he said anything that would get me to change my mind.

Grant took me to Shannon Airport and was kind enough not to ask too many questions. When he dropped me off, he told me to let them know if they could help in any way. I gave him a hug and told him to kiss Molly and Renae for me. I rushed into the airport and got in line to check-in. After a few minutes, I reached the desk, got my boarding pass and handed over my checked bag. I didn't really care if it made it on time. I got through security, which was a bit of a mess since my bag wasn't actually organized and made it to the gate.

Maeve called while I was waiting for the plane. She had just landed and was waiting at baggage claim. I apologized about having to close the shop and leave but she stopped me. She told me everything was going to be okay and not to worry about them. She told me to just get home and do what needed to be done. She told me I was welcome back anytime I wanted to visit and not to be a stranger. She also wanted updates about my dad. I thanked her for everything and told her I was so sorry we didn't get a proper goodbye. She told me it was 'bye for now' not 'bye forever' and she would see me again someday. They had gotten tickets for the train and would relax on the ride home and not to worry about them. Sean was going to try to make it. I told her I wished he wouldn't. It was still raining and the drive wouldn't be safe if he was speeding. She agreed but said Sean would do what he needed to and no one could tell him otherwise.

I hung up with Maeve and waited, numb with worry. When they called out to start boarding the plane, I waited as long as I could, but Sean didn't make it. I was half-relieved and half-forlorn. I wanted one last kiss but didn't want to have to say goodbye. The last person in line, I lingered, still hoping. Just as I resigned myself that I wouldn't see him and headed to the counter to scan my boarding pass, I heard my name. I looked at the woman at the counter and she locked eyes with me. She nodded her head once and started smacking the scanner against her other hand.

She looked at her co-worker. "Caoimhe, this silly thing isn't working again!" They both smiled at me. I turned and saw Sean in the terminal, heading my way. A security guard with a smile on his face was following him. He had me in his arms before I could blink. It felt so good. The rest of the world disappeared. I started to ask how he had gotten here so fast but he stopped my mouth with a long, deep kiss. We poured all our love into that kiss. It was both hello and goodbye, both sweet and wonderful, and powerful and full of yearning. We held each other tight, hoping it would never end.

It could have been seconds or hours later, someone softly cleared their throat. We broke from our trance, tears in our eyes.

I looked at Sean, "I have to go."

"This isn't over," he said softly, looking me in the eyes.

"I love you," I said and kissed him again. "I have to go." One more kiss, he told me he loved me, and I walked to the plane, my heart breaking. I looked back to see him watching me. I tried to smile. The security guard rested his hand on Sean's shoulder and they turned to leave.

I had to pay a little extra but I got into one of the first rows in economy. It was the middle seat but I didn't care, I had to get off the plane quickly because my layover wasn't that long. It was going to be an uncomfortable flight. Eleven hours of worry, about Dad, about Sean, about everything I had no control over. The whole world was spinning so fast, it didn't feel right to be sitting for so long. I broke out my e-reader but I couldn't seem to focus. I opened a blank document on my tablet and started to type a letter to my dad and then one to Sean. I filled both letters with love and told them both I didn't know what to do without them.

When what seemed like the longest, most cramped flight in the history of flights finally landed, I ran off the plane, squeaking into the gate just as they announced the last call for boarding. I didn't even have time to take my phone off airplane mode to check messages. I was so glad I made it, because the next flight to LA wasn't for another four hours. I should be touching down in less than three. I had a bit more room on that flight but that wasn't saying much. I was running on pure adrenaline and whatever snacks I could buy on the flight over. I couldn't tell you if they served a meal on the last flight or if I ate it. I do know that when the flight attendant walked by, I ordered two Jameson on the rocks and they were both gone in seconds. I think they followed that up with pretzels, again, I didn't know if I ate them or lost them somewhere in the seat back.

Arriving at LAX with all the hustle and bustle, I managed to keep my head long enough to find baggage claim and snag my bag. I turned on my phone as I left baggage claim and it blew up. I had to wait for the overwhelming buzzing to stop before I located, amongst all of them, a text from Sam that said she wasn't leaving Dad's side so Jake was coming to get me.

Jake made a few circles around the terminal waiting for me to get out of the airport. I texted him and he was just coming back around. He pulled up in front of me and I quickly threw my bag in the bed of his lor... I mean, truck and jumped in the passenger seat. I went through the thirty text messages from Mom, Sam, Jake, Sean, Maeve, and Molly. I weeded out the well wishes and the, "I'm going to miss you," texts and searched for updates on Dad. I finally put my phone down and looked at Jake. He had been quiet the whole time we had been in the truck. When he glanced over, he said it looked like I was all caught up and then filled me in on what was currently known. Jake drove us to the hospital and dropped me at the front door. He gave me directions and said he would park and be in.

I followed what he said, and once I got my visitors badge from the nurse's station, I found Dad's room. Sam was slumped over in a chair, her hand in his. Dad had all sorts of tubes around him and a bandage around his head. I touched her shoulder and she startled awake. I could see the confused emotions on her face. I enveloped her in a hug and she let go of all her emotions, her tears, and the past between them. I held her through her release, knowing I had to hold it together for her. I reached over and grabbed my dad's hand. It was warm. Once Sam relaxed and her crying subsided, I held her away from me and looked at her. I told her I was so sorry and pulled her in again.

Jake came in and I handed Sam over to him. I told Jake that I would stay and to take Sam home. She started to protest but I told her I would call her the minute something changed and to get some sleep and she could call me in the morning, and we would figure out a plan. I had some clothes in my backpack that wouldn't fit in my checked bag, so I had something to change into for tomorrow. Once they left, it was just me and Dad. I slid the chair that reclined next to Dad's bed and settled in for the night, reaching over and holding Dad's hand with my left hand and I sent a text to Sean with my right. He was upset, sad, and angry, also worried, hurt and resigned. I could read it all in the texts he sent me. He missed me. He knew that this was bound to happen but he wasn't happy about it or how it worked out. He was sorry about my dad and hoped he was okay. The whirlwind of emotions hit me and I muffled a cry. I held my knees and tried to quietly let out all the emotions I couldn't keep back any more.

At some point, I fell asleep, holding my phone and my Dad's hand. Sometime, around four in the morning, the night nurse came in to end her shift and do a final check on Dad's vitals. The morning nurse came in at about five in the morning, and at six a.m. sharp, the doctor came in to check and give me an update. He said they ran some tests and there shouldn't be any long-term issues that they could find from his fall and that it was just a waiting game to see when he would wake up.

Two days later, Dad started to stir. Sam and I were there playing cards over his lap. He recognized us but couldn't remember what happened. Sam crept carefully into his arms as I explained what I knew. He held Sam with one arm and reached for my hand. He said he was sorry to both of us that he wasn't there for us growing up. He told us he always wanted the best for us but just didn't know how to provide it. Sam started crying softly on his chest and my eyes teared up. He looked at me and said he was so proud of the woman I had become and that I always took such great care of my mother and sister, especially after he left. He apologized for leaving that burden on me and started crying too. I leaned in and hugged them both, thinking of Sean and how he would have done anything for me. The three of us cried softly in each other's arms.

The nurse came in quietly and apologized for interrupting. She said she would be back with the doctor soon.

The doctor said Dad could be released after they ran a few tests to make sure there were no cognitive delays, but he would need help at home until he had fully recovered. I offered to stay with Dad since I still had time off and I had the ability to be there full time. We got him home and settled. Sam and Jake stayed at my apartment and I stayed with Dad.

38

After some time, Sean and I fell into a pattern of talking when we could. I continued to stay with my dad and started to go back to work, getting in visits with Mom, and phone calls and texts to Ireland when I could. Sam and Jake stayed in my apartment which had really become their apartment since Sam made arrangements to pay a little extra rent to have a couple of animals. I wasn't interested in my apartment any more anyway. Mom distracted herself with wedding planning, we would talk, and I would go see her often. I felt like a robot. I was doing what I needed to for everyone but wasn't finding what I was looking for here.

Dad got better after a few months of physical therapy and I decided to start looking for a new apartment instead of kicking Sam and Jake out of my old apartment. I tried for something small so it wouldn't feel so empty.

After about two months of searching, a small apartment opened up in the same complex as my old one. Sam and Jake were excited that I would be so close. I thought about Sean often and wondered what he was up to. I had left a little more than five months ago; he had probably moved on or at least I told myself that. We would still text like nothing had changed and I missed him, I missed being in his arms, but at some point, he would move on and find someone else. Right? The ache in my heart hoped not but my head told me that it would happen.

I made arrangements with the apartment complex manager to come sign the paperwork for the new apartment. I stopped by Sam and Jake's place beforehand to see if there was any furniture I wanted to take to the new apartment. They were nowhere to be found. I still had the key so I let myself in and started to make a small list at the kitchen table of the things I wanted to take with me. It was mostly my books and shelves and my bed. Sam could keep everything else.

A few minutes later, I heard Sam and Jake get home, so I finished writing down mattress on the list as they came through the door. I start to turn around and make a smart-ass comment about them being MIA and there, standing before me was the redhead from my dreams… It was Sean. He was in jeans and a button-down with a cap in one hand and lilies wrapped in plastic in the other.

I blinked to make sure he was real, dropped my pen and raced into his arms. Sam must have taken the flowers and the hat because his fingers were in my hair. We kissed deeply and I almost forgot we weren't alone. Jake made a small noise and I pulled back a little, breaking our kiss.

I said, "I assume you've met my sister and Jake?" Sean wouldn't take his eyes off me but smiled and nodded.

"Aye, I have."

We stared at each other and a few minutes passed. Sean took a step back and I heard Sam gasp. Sean dropped to one knee and pulled out a small white box. He told me life didn't make sense after I left and that I was all he could think about. He said he expected it would be a couple of years before the wedding but he wanted me in his life forever and he couldn't imagine spending another day without me. Then he asked me to marry him.

I closed the gap between us and said that we had so much to figure out, but yes, of course, I would marry him. He kissed me deeply and I heard clapping around us. I broke eye contact and looked around. Both my parents were there, along with Sam and Jake. Sam came over and hugged me, saying that the proposal was not how they had planned it but then smiled and said it was better! We got a big group hug and I couldn't believe it, but my parents even smiled at each other. Sean put the ring on my finger. It was a Claddagh with little shamrocks on the cuffs of the hands that held the heart. The shamrocks matched my necklace. Sean said he bought it the same day.

A few weeks went by and I never did sign that lease. Family got used to the idea and we ultimately decided that we would both be happiest in Ireland. We moved my things from California into his house in Ireland. It was mostly my clothes and my books. While I was gone, he turned the last bedroom into a library.

He brought the last box in and set it down next to me. He wrapped his arms around my waist and hugged me close, lifting me slightly off the ground.

"I've loved you from the beginning, you know," he said as he looked into my eyes.

I smiled, kissed his nose, and said, "And I will love you till the end."

Epilogue

I squeezed my eyes shut, taking a deep breath. I opened them, looking down at the bouquet of flowers in my hand. Mom had found tiny green books with Shakespeare's sonnets at an antique store and had incorporated them in with the orchids, stephanotis blossoms, and the baby's breath. The delicate lace sleeves of my dress kept the morning chill from making me shiver.

I could hear the birds in the forest singing softly as the music began. My dad touched my elbow and told me it was time. He was in a steel grey suit with a Kelly green pocket square, smiling at me. We walked slowly, in time with the music. Sam was just ahead of me in a Kelly green satin dress, baby bump just starting to show. She had found out she was pregnant a couple of months after she and Jake had married.

Grant was in front of her with Renae in his arms. They turned the corner, walking into the prayer house in the forest and he set her down. He handed her a flower girl basket full of flower petals, straightened her white, fluffy dress, and pointed at Molly at the end of the aisle. Renae took a handful of petals from her basket and threw them at her feet then ran to her mom with the rest of the petals blowing out as she went. I laughed when I heard her say, "Mama, I did it!" Grant, Molly, and Renae quickly sat as

Sam walked down the aisle. Dad and I paused at the doorway. I could see Maeve and Tom, my mom, and George and his wife, Miriam sitting on the benches. We couldn't invite everyone to the ceremony because the prayer house was so small.

The music changed, dad kissed my hair, patted my hand on his arm and we walked in. Sean had his head down with his hands clasped in front of him. He was so handsome in his light grey suit with one of the green books mom had turned into a boutonniere with baby's breath around it on his lapel. Henry, his best friend, who came down from Westport, placed his hand on Sean's shoulder and Sean looked up. We locked eyes, I saw him take a deep breath, his bottom lip quivered, and he looked up for a second, finding some composure. I took a deep breath and he looked back at me with a winning smile that warmed me from my core. I smiled back, holding back tears.

I made it to the vows before those tears finally broke through. I practically whispered the words, dabbing my happy tears with the handkerchief that Maeve had added to the bottom of my bouquet. The priest pronounced us man and wife and we sealed the ceremony with a kiss that could have stopped time. Then he introduced us as the new Mr. and Mrs. Sean Alexander O'Bryan.

The reception at Ashford Castle, in one of the secluded gardens, had more people. Friends and family from back in the U.S. that could make the trip as well as Sean's side of the family and everyone from Cong. Arthur and Siobhan came with their three children as well as the staff from the castle.

We sat and laughed and ate and danced in the garden. We stayed as long as we could before the weather turned to clouds and a misty drizzle started to fall a few hours later. Sean and I walked hand-in-hand to the castle, through the moist air with our family and friends. We kissed and hugged everyone goodbye, or goodbye for now, as we would see most of them at the Crow's Nest in a couple of hours for drinks.

Sean wrapped his arms around me from behind after the last guest left.

"So, Mrs. O'Bryan, whatever should we do with ourselves now?" he whispered in my ear.

"I can think of a few things." I said as I turned in his arms. I kissed him on the nose and walked slowly up the stairs to the honeymoon suite.

All the thanks:

First to you, for taking the time to read my book.

To my husband, Adam, for his unyielding and steadfast support throughout the process of writing and his patience with my ever-changing moods depending on what my characters were going through. I love you.

To my mom, Bernadette, for her unwavering belief in me.

To my aunt, Francesca, for letting me work through my thoughts and giving me feedback and encouragement.

To Madeline and Will Newcombe, for indulging me on crazy adventures that gave me a break from writing and added details to the book I could never have gotten without them.

To Michael, Erika, Matthew and Nicholas Arrington for being my very own cheering section.

To Leilah Kelsey for coming forward when I really needed a new set of eyes and a different perspective.

To Samantha Rose for being the first to say I could use your name.

A big thank you to family and friends for all the encouragement and for asking for updates that kept me going.

And to everyone who told me I could do it. There are little bits of each of you in all my characters. I love you all.

Printed in the USA
CPSIA information can be obtained
at www.ICGtesting.com
CBHW030445260824
13582CB00054B/1224